Silvia's Smile

Diana Nicolaci

Nature holds everything to account, a tree grows from a seedling, its roots grow deep into the earth, its trunk and branches grow towards the light.

To many it seems as though the tree just exists, but to the tree it observes all the seasons. It soaks up and witnesses everything that surrounds it.

Once it has had its fill, it slowly implodes withers and disperses the memory of what it beheld back into the earth.

It allows time to pass until new shoots sprout from the seeds of the past, drawing the past into the present for another chance of bringing truth to light.

Chapter 1

Creeping down the dimly-lit passage, Silvia trembled, her heart raced as she moved closer to the sounds. Had someone broken in? She could feel the adrenalin rush through her body, giving her a heightened awareness. Her eyes adjusted to the faint light filtering through the curtains from the moonlight. She glimpsed the outline of a figure on the dining room table. Blinking a few times she sighed with relief. It was only Molly, her cat.

A ghastly moan came from the back room, in an instant she was once again racked with fear. As quietly as she could, she tiptoed toward the room; the door was slightly ajar so she gently pushed it open.

Standing there, silently, she tried to process what she was seeing. There was a mysterious light stealing through a crack in the floorboards. She could hear tapping and moved closer to investigate. Was someone beneath the floor?

She saw an axe leaning against the wall, grabbed it and plunged it into the floorboards. Raising it above her head, she swung it down, again and again, until the floorboards split open. Getting down on her hands and knees, she began clawing away at the chips of wood, her nails breaking as blood dripped from her fingers. Molly was beside her now, scratching at the floor.

Everything went silent; she peered down through the splintered boards. She was about to vomit from the fear. A duffle bag covered in dust was in the hole. Trembling, she reached down to grab it, pulling it to the surface. What was inside? Trying to unzip it she pushed and pulled, the blood dripping from her fingers helped to lubricate it. The zip gave way, and she opened it with shaking fingers.

'Nick,' Silvia gasped. 'Nick, Nick!' tears rolling down her cheeks, 'Nick, help me!'

Nick jerked awake and instinctively he pulled Silvia towards him and hugged her close. He reassured her, 'You're safe honey, calm down, I'm here.' Nick stroked her hair and kissed her.

Silvia fell into his arms sobbing, 'Oh God, Nick, I've had a terrible nightmare.'

Chapter 2

Still rattled from her nightmare, Silvia tried to focus on getting ready for her interview. She inhaled as she draped her cardigan over her left arm. If the people interviewing her saw her tattoo, she may not be offered the position. To work for a cosmetic surgeon, you would have to encourage people to hate their imperfections, not to love them.

Strangely, she was drawn to this position at a clinic where people would be coming in to have Botox and lip fillers, tummy tucks and wanting to alter their looks, yet Silvia believed people should accept their natural beauty. Had she placed herself into a bit of a conundrum? They probably wouldn't give her the job if they knew how she felt about cosmetic surgery, but she was good at hiding her feelings. She could push them down deep inside and no-one would know how she really felt.

That morning she decided to wear some black leggings; with a cute pair of short boot style heels which she had bought in Germany the previous year. The trip was to celebrate their wedding anniversary. They travelled the Rhine on a cruise from Amsterdam to Budapest. They had laughed to find they were the youngest couple on board. In hindsight, it was something they should have done for their 50th anniversary, rather than their 25th.

She paired the boots with a black wrap dress and a lacy pink scarf, taking one more look in the mirror before taking up her keys and running out the door.

Silvia was slender and petite, and very attractive for her age. Her hair was mousy coloured blond which she kept just below shoulder length, her eyes pale green. She had a small scar under her cheek that gave the appearance of a dimple, a childhood accident thanks to her brother playing sling shot. By the age of 47 so many woman had already dabbled in cosmetic surgery or at least had Botox. But not Silvia, she never intended to go down that road. She maintained her health and sanity through her art work, yoga and walking, and 3 or 4 glasses of wine every night.

Silvia had a slight Swedish accent which she tried hard to hide. Others found her accent interesting and sexy, but she didn't like it.

It was boredom that caused Silvia to browse the internet seeking a more interesting job than her current one. She would only apply if it was closer to home and offered a better salary. It also had to be cushier than the job she was in.

She was fed up with working for surgeons who double and triple booked their patients. The whole medical profession was causing her to feel despondent. Every place she had worked was so drab, with dull cream walls that could do with a lick of paint, and staff who had lost interest in caring for the patients. Perhaps it was because the GPs and surgeons were too stingy to spend a dollar on sprucing up their clinics? The places she had worked were definitely not conducive to health and happiness. If she had to be couped up all day working, she made a conscious decision that her next workplace would be a bright modern environment.

The advertisement for a medical receptionist position jumped out at her; it listed many of the things she desired. It was less than an 8 kilometre drive from her home; which would be a bonus because the traffic was getting worse by the day. The location of her current job was only 15 kilometres from her house but in the direction of the city which in peak hours meant the traffic was horrendous, and coming home was even worse. The cosmetic surgeon position was in the other direction, with far less traffic.

She pondered working for a cosmetic surgeon, and concluded it would have to be more fun and exciting than seeing people come in every day with haemorrhoids and bowel complaints.

Silvia was delighted but not surprised when she received a call asking her to come in for an interview.

The reception area was like walking into a high class hotel foyer, only smaller. There was a beautiful arrangement of flowers sitting in an artesian vase on the counter. On the wall behind the reception was a large motif of what looked like an Islamic design. Silvia was admiring it, when a tall stunning woman with flaming red hair appeared behind the counter.

'Can I help you?' she asked in a cheery voice.

'I hope so, I'm Silvia, and I'm here for an interview.'

'Oh lovely, just take a seat in the waiting room,' her face split into a Julia Roberts smile as she gestured in the direction of the waiting room.

'Thank you.' Silvia turned and sat down.

The red-head disappeared into another room, returning a moment later. Humming one of Adele's latest songs, she sat behind the reception desk.

Silvia liked what she saw; yes, this was exactly the type of place she had dreamed of working. The surroundings were like something out of an interior design magazine compared to other workplaces. Her eyes were drawn to the objects displayed on the glass topped coffee table. Two large glossy books, one with Marilyn Monroe on the cover and the other one in an opulent French-style prop was titled 'Coco Chanel.'

A crystal vase of pale pink ranunculus flowers completed the table display. The waiting room chairs were made of white leather and black satin cushions studded with crystal buttons were displayed on each chair. Along the back wall was a black leather couch and an original painting of a woman's silhouette hung above it.

Silvia wondered how many other people had applied for the position. Checking her watch, she realised she was 10 minutes early. They must be interviewing other people, she thought.

While waiting, Silvia reminisced about her first job. She recalled searching through the Herald/Sun newspaper, flipping through to the back pages where all the employment advertisements were listed. She found an ad – Melbourne Haberdashery - Receptionist wanted. Full Time Position. Must have Excellent Phone Skills and be able to Type 65-75 words per minute. Youth Wages Apply.

Silvia dialled the number from a nearby pay phone. The man who answered told her he already had enough people apply, and he had begun interviewing. Silvia wouldn't take no for an answer. He relented and asked her to come in the following day. Nearing the end of the interview, he informed her he would have to consult with his brother who was a partner in the business, and would get back to her the following day if she was successful.

Silvia said she needed to know soon because she had received another job offer. It was a lie, of course, but she thought it was a good way to manipulate him. It paid off because right there and then he told her she had the job. Later, she found out about his brother's annoyance at him for overstepping his authority.

She worked for the two Jewish brothers for about 3 years. They owned a haberdashery on Flinders Lane which nowadays is one of the trendy areas in Melbourne, but at that time it was the hub of the garment trade. Silvia lived in Dandenong, and had to commute to work on public transport.

She caught the train from Dandenong Station to Flinders Street Station. It took about an hour to get there, so she would knit to pass the time or read the Herald/Sun newspaper. It was in the 70s when people knitted and read newspapers and where there was a ticket booth where you could actually buy your ticket from a person, not a ticket machine.

Silvia loved to people watch, closely studying their faces and reactions. She would smile at them to see if they would smile back, some would return the smile, but others would pretend they didn't see her and turn the other way while others didn't show any expression or emotion at all. Maybe she was being too judgmental? She wondered if she was showing signs of parochialism. Maybe they were going through something shitty in their lives and she shouldn't judge them?

The haberdashery was a three story building with one level underground and two above. As the reception was underground she didn't have a window which bothered her. It was like being shut in a cage which made the day drag horribly.

Silvia probably would have worked at the haberdashery even longer except for one of the brothers making a smart remark about a boyfriend she was dating at the time. She couldn't remember exactly what he said but it was enough for her to make up her mind to leave.

'Hello, you must be Silvia?' Silvia quickly snapped out of her daydream and sprang up.

'It's nice to meet you, I'm Kerri Anne,' she held out her hand to shake Silvia's.

'Yes, I'm Silvia, it's nice to meet you too,' Silvia replied.

'Sorry for making you wait; we are running a little behind.'

'Oh, that's fine.' Silvia chirped.

Was Kerri Anne of Spanish decent? Her thick brown hair flowed over her shoulders and down her back. She was wearing tight black leather-look pants with stiletto shoes and a cream chiffon shirt.

'Follow me into my office and I'll introduce you to the practice manager.'

She followed her in. Silvia was impressed with Kerri Anne's appearance and professional manner, although she came across as slightly arrogant. She couldn't help but be impressed at the continuation of the white, light interior design of these rooms. A black and white painting of a nude woman lying on her side was on the back wall. Two glass-framed photos of a boy and a girl sat on the desk, no doubt, her children. For once in her life, Silvia felt overwhelmed with the luxe style and glamour of the people and the place.

A woman was sitting in front of the desk and looked up as they entered. She was 45, maybe 50 years of age. Her face told the story. She obviously had taken advantage of the cosmetic treatments, perhaps surgery, which were their stock and trade. Her face was stretched and frozen which gave her inanimate appearance. Nothing moved on her face which lacked any expression. She seemed nice enough as she nodded a hello.

'This is Sally, Sally is the practice manager and I am the operations manager,' Kerri Anne explained.

'Lovely to meet you,' Silvia reached out to shake Sally's hand.

Silvia was directed to a chair to the right of Sally while Kerri Anne walked around her desk and sat down.

They took it in turns to question her. They were the usual questions like why did she want to leave her current job, and why did she think she would like working for a cosmetic surgeon. They went on to create a scenario of a difficult client and asked her how she would deal with complaints which she handled surprisingly well. She had dealt with a few troublesome patients and customers in her previous jobs.

The interview seemed to go well. Silvia answered their questions easily, and was calm and in control. At this point in her life, she didn't really care if she was offered the job or not. If she was meant to get the position, she would. The fact that she didn't really care seemed to be the key to Silvia getting any job she wanted. It was as though people were drawn to her because of her un-neediness.

'Thank you for coming in, we will get back to you within the next day or two. We have two more people to interview,' said Kerri Anne.

'No problem, it was lovely to meet you both,' replied Silvia.

Silvia had the support of her husband; her life didn't depend on getting this job, although she was treading water and becoming more bored and restless as the weeks went on. She definitely needed a change.

Secretly, Silvia had always wanted to start her own business teaching people creative art work. Painting had become a sort of escapism for her and it was the main reason she had become more content in her life. Deep down, Silvia wanted to help others find enjoyment and escapism in the same way she had.

Chapter 3

Silvia's best friend, Rita, was waiting for her in the car. Poor Rita was caught in an abusive relationship with a womanizing jerk. Only God knew why she put up with him. Rita's background was Russian; she was a little taller than Silvia. She coloured her hair a reddish burgundy which she kept at shoulder length and had professionally straightened every week. She liked to wear nice clothes and it was true that men found her sexy, not only because of her Russian accent but also because of her voluptuous body.

Rita had been dating Frank for six years but Silvia felt a strong antipathy towards him. The first time Silvia met him she sensed something wasn't quite right about him. Just the fact he was in his mid-forties and didn't have a cracker to his name rang alarm bells. She never voiced her opinion to Rita because it really was none of her business.

She was about to open the door of her car, when she noticed Rita sitting there. 'What are you doing in the driver's seat?'

'If you don't mind, I'd like to drive. I've been thinking of buying a car like this and wanted to get the feel of driving it.'

'OK, no problem.' Silvia shrugged her shoulders and laughed as she walked around the car to the passenger door.

'I didn't know you were thinking of buying a new car?'

'Well my car is getting old, it's about time I bought a new one. Anyway, how did the interview go, Silv?'

'If I get it, I get it and if I don't, bad luck I suppose.'

Silvia had passed the stage of really wanting anything; she knew it was all in the hands of the universe.

'Exactly Silv, if they don't give you the position it's their loss.' Rita laughed and Silvia joined in with her.

Silvia and Rita had planned to have lunch that day at Rosie's, their favourite restaurant. It worked out perfectly because Silvia's interview was an hour before their lunch date. Rita had nothing better to do that day, so she sat in the car with the windows down, reading. Rita loved to read romance and mystery novels, but occasionally she would read the odd biography.

While she was driving, Rita told Silvia about the book she was currently reading. The author was David Icke and she explained that he had a strange spiritual experience in Peru or somewhere, and the royal family are reptilians, and that subliminal messages are everywhere in advertising, sexual in nature, because sex sells.

'Take a look,' Rita gestured to Silvia to pick up the book that was sitting on top of her bag.

'Turn to the page with my bookmark in it.'

Silvia turned to the page, there was a picture of a man's abdomen, an advertisement for men's after shave. The muscles in his stomach were shaped into a huge penis; you couldn't see it at first until it was pointed out.

Silvia turned to her, 'Wow, I see it, the book sounds interesting Rita, I mean you know me, I'm open-minded, but I wouldn't be going around telling people that you believe in this kind of stuff. They would definitely think you're crazy, I mean, yeah the subliminal messages, I can see it could be true, but the royals and reptilians, sounds off-the-planet way out.'

Rita was a little crazy which was one of the things Silvia liked about her. She wasn't boring, that's for sure.

When they arrived at Rosie's, the waitress made sure they were seated at the best table. She knew them both by name, Rita had made sure of that, she was loud and outgoing whereas Silvia was more reserved. Rosie's was popular, a favourite place for women to meet for a mid-week lunch. You saw the occasional businessman in a suit, sitting with an attractive woman or a client they were trying to impress. Frequently, there were groups of women celebrating someone's birthday; you knew it because of the little gifts or flowers presented to the blushing birthday girl. 'Oh you shouldn't have!' they would gush.

One of Rosie's best features was the outdoor seating area with comfortable lounge type chairs and a fountain on the wall for ambiance. The outdoor area was utilised summer and winter, with umbrellas for summer and plastic blinds and heaters for winter. The interior of the restaurant was just as pleasant with an electric log fireplace with simulated flames that was inviting on a cold day. It was decorated with fine art and was light and airy. Local produce was for sale at the counter, not too much, just some jams and essential oils. As it was nestled between a lakeside park and some townhouses, Rosie's was inviting for the locals, especially the ones who jogged around the lake, then stopped in for a coffee.

They had a good lunch deal going: for $19.95 you could select from a menu of five dishes with a house wine or a coffee included.

It was a breezy day so the waitress directed them inside to a table under a window with a view of the lake. Silvia decided on the mushroom risotto and Rita wanted the same but with chicken and no cream, she always had to be a little difficult. Silvia just ordered from the menu, but Rita always had to make a little change, such as no cream, or she would ask "What spices does it have in it? I'm not sure that spice would agree with me."

Did she do it just to keep the kitchen and the waitresses on their toes, or maybe she did it for attention. Whatever the reason, it embarrassed Silvia. It didn't bother Rita who had a way with words. Most people liked her. Even when it came to ordering the wine, Rita would have to ask, is it from South Australia or Victoria? Silvia was happy with the house wine, any wine in fact, but Rita had to make sure of the region it was grown. In the end, she decided on the house wine because it was included in the lunch deal, and it wasn't too bad after all.

As the waitress bought the wine to the table, Rita's phone rang; she fumbled around trying to find it in her oversized bag. 'It's Frank,' she whispered as she stood up to take the call outside.

Silvia watched as Rita walked away. Her hair was swaying to and fro and her hands were gesturing like she was trying to explain some intricate detail. Silvia sat pondering whether she should start without her. She decided to wait hoping the call wouldn't take too long. She studied her wine glass and was happy the waitress had filled it a little over the standard drink mark. She hated it when they poured it just under, or exactly at the mark. Usually, she would click a cheers with Rita but she couldn't be bothered waiting. Just as she was bringing the glass to her lips, Rita came back to the table looking flustered.

Silvia put the glass down, 'What's up, Rita?'

'Oh, he just wanted to know what I'm doing and who I'm with, it was nothing, you know how it is.'

No, I don't know how it is. He's trying to control you, Silvia thought but she bit her tongue and shrugged her shoulders. How could Rita not see that Frank was a jerk? At least she didn't have to put up with him, at least Nick wasn't like Frank.

'Oh and guess what, I just saw Nick outside, I asked him to join us but he said he only popped in for a coffee, and didn't want to intrude.'

Rita's expression revealed her relief at the change of subject. She lifted her glass, 'Cheers, to friendship.'

'Oh really, I think he was seeing a client down the road from here; yes it slipped my mind, he told me he had a meeting with a client.'

Silvia contemplated telling Rita about her nightmare, but she knew she couldn't be completely honest with her. Knowing Rita, she would ask too many questions, and Silvia wasn't prepared to answer them. There was a part of her that needed to talk about what had happened, to blurt out her anger, frustrations and fears but there was another part that knew she had to keep quiet. Rita was her best friend, but some things were best kept secret.

Silvia clicked her glass with Rita's, and soon they were enjoying their lunch, sipping wine and talking about the job Silvia was hoping to get.

Catching up with Rita was always fun. They would often go out for lunch or sometimes they would go and see a movie together at the Cameo Theatre in Belgrave, which showed more arty films. Surrounded by the Sherbrooke Forest at the foothills of the Dandenong Ranges, Belgrave was a quaint little suburb with some great cafes and unique shops they loved to frequent. After watching a movie, they would spend the rest of the day going in and out of different stores, rummaging through op shops and trying on second-hand clothes.

Sometimes they would see the wizard who lived up there, Baba Desi was his name, an old hippie character who often sat outside the cafes talking to the locals. He was a friendly old man who was probably in his eighties. He wore an eye patch and carried around a large walking stick that was bound up with colourful string and cloth. He had become a bit of an icon in Belgrave and people often asked if they could have a photo taken with him.

Silvia and Rita were close friends, but they were from very different backgrounds. Silvia had developed a strong personality, to the point of being tough-minded when she had to be. Her childhood was harsh; she had a dominating mother who was a perfectionist and quick with the belt or anything else that came to hand when she was angry which she often was.

Silvia's father on the other hand was a quiet man. He was hard working, very aloof, and enjoyed his alcohol a little too much. He was more of a man's man, and although he provided financially, he never provided emotionally. He wasn't home much; he was either, working, or at the pub or out camping or hunting with his friends.

When they migrated from Sweden, Silvia was twelve. She found it difficult to leave her friends behind. It was as if her heart had been ripped out of her body. Since she was a small child, she had fitted into her home and community. In her brash new country of Australia, nothing fitted. She struggled to learn English and to make friends. As she grew older and was able to talk more with her mother, she realised the move to Australia had been even harder for her mother. It was the source of her frustrations which she took out on Silvia and her brother Ted.

Silvia was unable to have children of her own, so she resigned herself to being an aunty to her brother Ted's children. She had been the best aunty she knew how to be, and enjoyed it enormously. Her brother had three children; Charlotte who was 26 and living with her boyfriend in an upmarket town house in St Kilda; Jarrod, 25, who loved to travel, and was currently on a surfing holiday in Bali; and Phoebe who was 23 and five months pregnant to a scumbag who deserted her as soon as he found out she was pregnant. Ted's children loved Silvia like their own mother. Their mother had died of breast cancer when they were very young and Ted never remarried. He dated a few women but could never commit to any of them.

On the other hand, Rita was an only child and her parents had doted on her. Perhaps that's why Rita had chosen jerks? Maybe it was because she had everything given to her on a silver platter, and it was her way of rebelling? Rita had been married but the marriage ended in a divorce. She found out her husband was having a love affair - *with golf* - and she just couldn't compete. So as soon as her son turned 16, she was out. She figured that her husband and her son could take care of each other.

Silvia liked to analyse everything. She was a bit of a self-help junkie. She had read Louise Hay's book, "You Can Heal Your Life" countless times, and thought she had the answers to everyone else's problems. It was easy for her to know what other people should do although she didn't know how to erase her own demons. The past couldn't be changed, all she could do was try to forget her past and move forward.

****

Three days after the interview Silvia received a call from Kerri Anne. 'Hello, Silvia, this is Kerri Anne, we would like to offer you the position. We feel you would be an asset to our practice. Can you come in tomorrow to meet with Jim Istible, the cosmetic surgeon?'

Chapter 4

As Silvia parked, it was impossible to miss a red BMW series 8 convertible, number plates MAGNET. It had to be Jim Istible's car.

Silvia was wearing an outfit she had bought from Ishka, a Bohemian style dress with swirling brown and olive green patterns with a hint of burgundy. She paired the dress with brown leather heels. She teased her hair to give it some volume, and after trying several attempts to put it up, she decided it looked better out.

Silvia had been offered and accepted the position, so this meeting was only a formality. She wasn't too worried about her appearance today; she felt confident and wanted to be more relaxed. He was probably an old fuddy duddy anyway, she thought to herself. Most of the surgeons she had worked for were very uninteresting.

She glanced in her rear-view mirror, rummaged in her bag and found her lipstick, applying a fresh coat of pink lip-gloss. With a wink of approval, she was ready to meet Jim Istible.

Within a couple of minutes of meeting him, Silvia could tell Jim Istible had taken an instant liking to her. His eyes travelled greedily down and up her body, lingering on her breasts for longer than was decent. She liked knowing that men found her attractive, and enjoyed his attention.

'Lovely to have you on board, Silvia,' Jim reached out to shake her hand. 'I'm Jim Istible as in irresistible.' He gave a little chuckle.

Silvia inwardly chuckled to herself. He thinks of himself as an irresistible MAGNET, remembering the number plates. 'That must be your car I saw outside with the number plates MAGNET,' she replied.

Jim laughed, 'I like a girl who takes notice of her surroundings.'

'Well it's quite an impressive car, irresistible even,' she flirted back.

Silvia calculated that he was in his fifties. He had so much Botox injected into his face that he reminded her of one of those puppets from that old show "The Thunderbirds." She could tell he was in the process of having a hair transplant, because of the beading tuffs of hair, placed in rows, like the ones that the old style dolls have. He must be midway through the procedure, Silvia guessed. He had an infectious smile with a mouth full of larger than life bright white teeth. There was something about him that Silvia liked, power perhaps?

'My thoughts exactly. Now let's get down to business. My expertise is in boobs, they call me the boob man. Of course I do other procedures like facelifts and tummy tucks, but I love doing boobs the most.'

As he spoke, he didn't make eye contact with her. Strangely, he stared, unblinking, at his phallic Egyptian carving on his desk. 'The women who come in for boob jobs always leave happy. Not like people who come in for nose jobs, you can never please them. I decided not to do them anymore because I couldn't convince some pernickety clients that their noses weren't the problem. But boobs, that's where the money is. I hope you don't have any issues with cosmetic surgery?'

'No, none at all,' replied Silvia, shaking her head to emphasise the point. But deep down she did, she believed people had to love themselves exactly how they were, which was why she had the reminder tattooed on her inner forearm:

Love the imperfections

'Come, I'll introduce you to the rest of the team,' Jim bounced up from behind his desk and they walked into the main reception area.

'This is Pamela, the office manager.'

Office manager, thought Silvia, wasn't Kerri Anne the operations manager and Sally the practice manager; how many managers were there in this small practice?

'Oh yes, I met Pamela when I came in for the interview.'

Pamela was the attractive red-head at reception.

'And this is Melissa, she's our theatre bookings girl,' Melissa was a chubby lady, probably in her late 30s or early 40s with a friendly personality.

'Welcome Silvia, you'll love working here.' Melissa's face lit up as she acknowledged Silvia.

'You'll meet the rest of the team when you start. You're happy with the days we want you to work, Monday to Thursday and every second Saturday with every Friday off ?'

'Yes, perfect,' replied Silvia.

'We need you to start in a month's time, is that OK with you?'

'Yes, Sally explained that to me in the initial interview.'

'Great I'll see you then, Pamela, can you show Silvia around?' Jim shook Silvia's hand, gestured for Pamela to take over and disappeared into his office.

Pamela gave Silvia a quick overview regarding the running of the practice. Her role was to sit at front desk and greet patients, take their details and bill them, very basic reception duties. It was going to be a pretty cushy job, exactly what Silvia wanted.

'I won't bother you with too much information now. When you start, we can go through everything one step at a time.'

'Thanks so much, I'm looking forward to it.' Silvia left the clinic feeling excited and couldn't wait to tell Nick about her new job and the interesting characters who worked there.

Chapter 5

Nick had arranged for them to go into the city that evening to celebrate. He didn't tell her what he had planned; only that it was a surprise and he was taking her out for dinner.

As far as Silvia was concerned, Nick was a Greek God. He was tall and handsome with strong masculine features. After all these years together, she still felt that sensation of excitement when he kissed her even though sometimes the sex was predictable. At other times, Nick would surprise her and want to try something different. Occasionally he shocked her but Silvia was open minded and tried different things, at least once anyway.

Like the time he wanted to try golden showers, she never really understood how that could turn anyone on, but Nick wanted to try it and it couldn't hurt to try. But no, she didn't think it was that exciting peeing on each other, it wasn't something she wanted to do again.

Nick's car pulled into the driveway; Silvia opened the front door and gave him a peck on the lips as he walked into the house. 'Hi honey, how was your day?'

'Good,' he replied putting down his briefcase. He walked into the kitchen and opened the fridge. 'One of our clients had the computer system crash so I spent the whole day sorting that out,' he said as he made himself a sandwich.

'Don't eat too much or you won't be hungry. You're taking me out for dinner tonight, aren't you?'

Turning around smiling, Nick pulled Silvia towards him, and hugged her. 'I haven't forgotten. How did the meeting go with the surgeon?'

'Really good, I think I'm going to like working there. The people seem fun. Jim, the surgeon, thinks of himself as an irresistible magnet, he has the number plates MAGNET, and his surname is Istible,' Silvia laughed.

'Really? What a tosser, and you honey, what do you think? Is he irresistible?' Nick asked jokingly.

'He has a certain charm.' Silvia replied with a mischievous grin.

Nick patted Silvia on the bum, as she turned away.

'I'll be in my art room for a while. You relax for a bit, oh and I've ironed some clothes for you to wear tonight. They're on the bed.'

Nick finished his sandwich, sat down and flicked through his phone for half an hour to wind down. He then showered while Silvia was in her art room arranging her paints and canvases.

It didn't take Nick long to get ready. He sat in the living room and flicked through the channels on the TV trying to find something of interest while he waited for Silvia.

'Silvia,' Nick called out from the living room, 'are you nearly ready? I've got a big night planned.'

'Yes I'm ready,' Silvia called back, spraying her favourite perfume, Angel, into the air in front of her and walked through the vapour. She had seen this technique on the Queer Eye for a Straight Guy show; they said it leaves a more subtle scent. She took a quick look in the mirror, and was pleased by what she saw. Her green eyes were accentuated with brown eye shadow and dark eyeliner and her soft neutral coloured lips on her tanned face made her look sexy.

She made her entrance into the living room. 'You look gorgeous,' Nick admired his wife. Her hair was out and she was wearing a pretty black dress with lacy straps and high heel stilettos.

'You don't look too bad yourself,' she teased. Nick was wearing camel coloured pants with a black lightweight bamboo shirt.

Nick had pre-booked parking online, as parking in the city could be a pain. The drive in was smooth and the night air was warm with a slight breeze. They had the radio on 106.7 PBS, they liked alternative music and Ai Du started playing from the album Talking Timbuktu with Ry Cooder. It was such a sexy song to be listening to while they drove.

After parking the car, Nick took Silvia by the hand and they walked down Exhibition Street. They arrived at a cocktail bar named Bar1806. Silvia loved the atmosphere right away; it was a chic little bar with dim lights and a stylish décor. A cute waiter directed them to the table Nick had reserved, he handed them both a cocktail menu and talked them through some of the cocktails on offer, and said he'd give them some time to make their choices.

There were small intimate tables scattered around, some with red velour chairs, others with brown leather chairs. It was crowded but not overly. The bar itself had small chandeliers hanging above it, and behind it was a large cabinet full of different bottles of alcohol and exquisite cocktail glasses.

Silvia looked through the list. 'This one looks interesting,' she commented, 'The 1806 Negroni,' and read aloud from the menu, 'The story goes that in 1919, one Italian Count Camillo Negroni, a regular customer at Casoni bar in Florence asked for his Americano cocktail to be made with more of a kick. The bartender Fosco Scarselli responded by taking out the soda water and replacing it with gin. It was this combination that became known as one of Count Negroni's drinks. After some time, the name of the cocktail was shortened to a Negroni – it has Tanqueray Gin – Martini Rosso – Campari and Orange Bitters. I'll try one of those, what are you going to have Nick?'

'I think I'll have a whiskey sour, no, no, a Manhattan,' Nick raised his hand to beckon the waiter, 'My beautiful wife would like to try a Negroni and I'll have a Manhattan,' Nick said with a cheeky grin.

'Good choices,' the waiter said with a slight bow of his head.

The music in the background was alternative and the place put Silvia into a dreamy state, 'I love it here Nick, I could stay here all night.' It wasn't long before their cocktails arrived.

'Cheers honey, to us.' Nick looked at Silvia and was pleased with himself for organizing the night.

Silvia raised her glass clicking it against Nick's, 'Cheers.'

They talked about Silvia's new job until she changed the subject and asked Nick about his new contract. Nick was a CS (computer scientist). His master's degree in science and mathematics and his interest in software design led him to a well-paid job, although he often had to travel, which he didn't really like.

'The contract they are offering is for another year and the great thing is I won't have to travel interstate, I have one initial trip to Germany but it will only be for a week, two at the most.'

'Wow that's great, Nick' Silvia beamed, her adoring gaze on him. Perhaps it was the Negroni making her feel chilled.

Nick looked at Silvia, she was aging but beautiful. There was a deep pain within him, a guilt that he couldn't escape. The past was something he wanted to forget, but every now and then he was reminded of it. When he was the most happy, he felt he didn't deserve to be. He quickly put it out of his mind, 'Come on, honey, finish your drink and let's go, I've got dinner planned and then something special.' He took her by the hand, leaving behind a generous tip for the waiter.

There was a hustle and bustle of people as they stepped out on the footpath. It was only a short walk from Bar 1806 to Gyoza Douraku, a Japanese Gyoza bar and restaurant. It was a small place with an authentic Japanese ambiance. Nick wanted to try something different to impress Silvia, a friend at work had recommended Gyoza Douraku to him.

Silvia and Nick selected a range of dumplings and tempura with some miso soup on the side. After their meal, it was time for Nick's surprise, he had arranged for them to go to the Marriott Hotel where they were ushered into an intimate room with about 50 guests. The sign at the front announced the event as, 'Impossible Occurrences,' a magic show.

Silvia looked up at Nick and gave him a quick kiss, 'Wow, this is fabulous,' she whispered. They enjoyed a night of bewilderment and charm and later on, making love when they returned home.

Chapter 6

Silvia woke at 3a.m. with excruciating pains in her chest, she thrashed about so violently, she fell out of bed, crying out, 'Nick, call an ambulance!' She was gasping for breath, rolling from side to side on the floor. Clutching her at her chest, Silvia curled up in a ball.

Nick jumped out of bed, his eyes bulging. 'What's wrong?'

Silvia screamed, 'I don't know, I think I'm having a heart attack, call an ambulance, quick Nick.'

Later, Silvia found out from Nick that it was his quick decision that saved her. She had slipped into unconsciousness. Nick refused to wait for an ambulance and bundled her into his car and drove at top speed to the hospital which was fortunately only 6 or 7 kilometres away from their house. Silvia could hardly breathe from the pain which was coming in waves.

Nick was standing beside Silvia who was now lying in a hospital bed in the emergency department. After having a morphine injection and some blood tests, a surgeon came in to give them the news.

'It's her gallbladder,' the surgeon explained, his eyes bloodshot and weary. 'The pain from a gallbladder attack can be mistaken for a heart attack, she will have to have emergency surgery as there is a stone obstructing the duct and her liver is being compromised.'

It was a funny thing that she was the one lying in the hospital bed because Nick looked as if he should be lying in one too. His face was drained of colour and deep shadows had appeared under his eyes.

Nick held her hand as the surgeon explained that it can be hereditary. Silvia remembered that her mother had her gallbladder removed in her early thirties.

****

The temple appeared desolate and barren to her. Had it been abandoned? Dust, cobwebs and darkness overshadowed it. But deep within, a dim light flickered. For some reason it seemed as though everything was running backwards. Silvia had come to this place, not knowing how she had found herself there. She peered through the temple gates and thought, "How is it so dark and empty?"

The light was growing brighter and in it she found a beacon of hope, there were signs of life. As she walked through the gates, she understood that the owner had abandoned this magnificent structure. Why was it abandoned? Was it attacked by an enemy? Were the people distracted? Perhaps they were forced to leave and build someone else's temple? What a shame, she could see the damage left behind, the damage of neglect, the damage of abuse and not caring, she could see that the owner had given up. There was a buildup of toxic waste, what a shame she thought.

But as she walked through into the next chamber, Silvia could feel a pulse, a slow but continuous beating like that of a heart. She unravelled the layers of silk and shook out the dust, which rose into the air and made her cough. She was angry that someone could be so careless, so distracted.

In the distance she saw the flickering. She walked towards it. As she came up close, she could see a lamp stand with three candles and above it was a photograph of the owner. Tears welled up inside her, how could she have been so blind?

****

There was a knock at the front door. Still a little unsettled from the vivid dream, she walked slowly down the hall. It had been 4 days since her surgery and she was still in a considerable amount of pain.

Two Jehovah's Witness Elders were standing there. She reluctantly opened the door.

'Hello Silvia, how have you been? We have missed you at the meetings,' they asked, speaking over each other.

Silvia had attended some of their meetings but had no intention of continuing, and now she didn't know how to get rid of them.

'Sorry I'm not feeling well; could you come back another time?' She really meant leave me alone, don't ever come back.

She hadn't been well for a long time, and her health took her on a journey of self-discovery. When she found out she couldn't have children, she felt as if she was being punished by God.

She immersed herself into religion and philosophy, but soon knew that religion wasn't a path she wanted to take. In her mind she didn't need a middle man; she could do her own research and talk to God herself.

Once the Jehovah's Witnesses left, she made herself a cup of tea and sat pondering the vivid dream. It left her feeling as though she hadn't been taking care of herself. She had been drinking a lot and not eating well; perhaps it was her way of dealing with the past but it was time she made changes. This dream wasn't a nightmare; it was a wake-up call.

She had to accept that she couldn't have children; endometriosis had left her with the need for a total hysterectomy and she and Nick didn't want to go down the road of surrogacy.

Here she was again, in pain, after yet another surgery. She decided the next time the Jehovah's Witnesses returned she would tell them the truth, that she wasn't interested.

Silvia was happy that she had time to recover before beginning her new job. She was looking forward to the change of environment.

Chapter 7

'Morning Silvia,' Pamela greeted her with a welcoming smile. She was wearing a smart-looking uniform, with black pants and a fitted black top with light blue piping along the pockets. Her name was embroidered below the logo of the clinic.

'Good morning,' Silvia replied, 'I love this reception area; it's so beautifully decorated'.

Pamela explained that Jim had expensive tastes and wanted only the best for his practice.

'This will be your desk, here at front Reception and mine is behind this divider. You can leave your bag under the desk. We ask that your phone is switched to silent at all times, and never let anyone see you on your phone at work.'

'Of course, Pamela,' replied Silvia.

'Oh and just call me Pam. Jim likes to call me Pamela but I'm happy with Pam. Do you like to be called Silvia or can we call you Silv, or Silly, only joking?'

'You can call me Silv, if you like,' Silvia laughed off the joke which she didn't find at all funny.

Silvia switched her phone to silent and placed her bag under the desk. She was taking it all in and admiring the beautiful white leather chair where she would sit. 'Classy, and comfy,' she thought.

'You will be fitted for a uniform in the next few days. What do you think of it?' Pam put her hand behind her head and, laughing, she paraded like a model.

'I love it, it's really modern,' replied Silvia.

'Yeah, we received this design recently; we like to change the design yearly. The last uniform was black pants with a blue top but we thought this time we would go with blue piping and embroidery.

Silvia nodded, and saw another staff member enter the room.

'Oh, this is Katy, our nurse,' said Pam, 'Katy, this is the new receptionist, Silvia.'

Katy had an air of importance about her; she was slim probably in her mid-thirties. She had chestnut brown hair cut into a bob and wore hardly any makeup. She was pale and had freckles on her cheeks and nose, which gave her a young appearance. She seemed to be in too much of a hurry to acknowledge Silvia, just giving her a quick nod before she rushed into one of the consulting rooms.

Pam explained, 'Katy is Jim's main nurse. He has other nurses but Katy is the one who consults with patients after Jim has seen them. She answers most of the questions they forget to ask him and she spends more time with them, explaining the procedures. You will know more once you've been here for a couple of weeks.'

Silvia nodded.

'Follow me, and I'll show you around and introduce you to the others.'

Pam knocked on the door of one of the consulting rooms, and opened it carefully, making sure there were no patients in the room. 'Claudia, this is Silv, the new girl who will be helping out in reception.' Pam turned to Silvia, 'This is Claudia, our Botox and fillers consultant.'

'Hi Silv,' Claudia said, smiling.

'Nice to meet you, Claudia,' replied Silvia.

Claudia was statuesque and striking in her looks. She turned heads. Her blond hair was cut into a short edgy style. She had a South African accent; she must have been from Dutch decent, perhaps third generation, concluded Silvia.

'It won't take you long to fit in, Silv, everyone is like family here, and if you want any Botox or fillers, just come see me,' she gave Silvia a nod and a wink.

Silvia laughed it off as a joke, because she had no intention of taking up the offer.

'And this is Judith.'

'Hello Silvia, lovely to meet you.'

'Judith is one of our nurses; she comes in to help now and then,' said Pam.

Judith was in Claudia's room, it looked as though Claudia must have just finished giving her some injections, because there were small bumps on the skin around her eyes and between her eyebrows.

Silvia took an instant liking to Judith who was older than the others, perhaps mid-50s. Her silver-coloured hair was pulled back into a short ponytail. She looked as though she had just been on a Mediterranean holiday because her skin had a deep glowing tan. It was Judith who later pulled Silvia aside and told her about the workings of the practice, that it was more than a little incestuous.

'Be careful Silvia, they are all related, and if they're not related, they are friends from way back. Keep your distance and you'll be fine,' she warned. Silvia placed that information into the back of her mind for the time being.

Pam proceeded to show Silvia where the tea room was and the powder room. Then she knocked on Melissa's door, 'You've already met Melissa, this is her office. I don't think she's in yet because she normally drops her kids off at school and arrives just after 9 o'clock.' Pam opened the door and showed Silvia the office. Melissa was definitely not a tidy person, there was paperwork all over the place and two or three used coffee cups on her desk, along with an old box of Krispy Cremes and a half eaten donut.

'She's messy,' laughed Pam, 'but she's fun to be around and does her job well.'

Pam spent the morning informing Silvia about the operations and procedures of the practice and how to use the computer system.

Silvia was taking it all in, nodding and agreeing with Pam. The people all seemed lovely. It was interesting to see the type of people who came in to see Jim Istible. They ranged from 18 year old girls wanting breast implants to older women wanting tummy tucks or facelifts, to middle aged men wanting Botox.

Silvia recognised one of the women who came in that afternoon as one of the local councillors; she spoke as though she had a plum in her mouth.

'Hello lovelies, it's that time again, can you believe it?' said the plum-in-mouth councillor.

'Has it already been 3 months? My, how time flies,' replied Pam.

'Yes, I tried to stretch it out to 4 months but I really needed my Botox treatment before my girlfriend's 40th.'

Pam and Melissa laughed and joked with her, as though they were long-lost friends. As soon as she walked out the door, they both bagged her, saying how obnoxious she was. Silvia thought it was hilarious. It was all so different from her previous positions. Silvia had worked with such high profile surgeons who were at the cutting edge of their fields. One of them was working on the bionic eye, and another was working on stem cell research into bowel reconstruction. It was a relief to work with people who were a little more fun and superficial.

Silvia started filing away the morning's patient files into the compactus. Whilst tucked away filing, she overheard Pam talking to Melissa about Sally, the practice manager.

'Did you know that Jim is taking her on a surprise holiday for her 50th birthday?' asked Pam.

'No I didn't, he's so good to her, she is so lucky,' said Melissa who sounded a little jealous of Sally.

'He was asking me for my opinion, on whether he should keep it a surprise or just tell her. He wants to take her to Paris.'

'Oh God, really?' replied Melissa.

Silvia emerged from the compactus and tried to pretend she hadn't heard a word although Pam and Melissa turned to Silvia and happily included her into the conversation. 'You know Sally is Jim's wife?' Pam queried.

'Oh, no I didn't,' replied Silvia.

Pam continued, 'Sally and Jim have been married for 25 years and they are still very much in love. She was working as a practice manager back in the day and that's how they met. She really helped him through a rough period in his life when his first wife left him.'

Silvia nodded and gave Pam what she hoped was an understanding look.

'Jim was devastated; apparently his ex had met a wealthy jeweller and told Jim she didn't love him anymore. She was a gold digger in every sense of the word,' laughed Pam.

'She ruined Jim emotionally and financially, but then Sally and Jim got together and built up this practice to where it is now.'

'Oh really,' Silvia was surprised by Pam's effortless sharing of such personal of information.

'Anyway, that's water under the bridge now. Sally is turning 50 at the end of this year, and Jim is surprising her with a trip to Paris. I suspect she will have a big birthday party as well, so mum's the word.'

'I never heard a thing,' laughed Silvia.

Pam went on to explain how she was Sally's best friend from way back and they had lived in the same street growing up.

'Oh I thought you seemed very close to Sally,' replied Silvia.

Pam nodded, adding, 'Melissa's my cousin, she was looking for work, and at the time we needed someone here, so it worked out well.'

Melissa butted in, 'When I started working here, I met Katy and realised that our kids go to the same school. It's a small world, hey?'

Silvia was beginning to put the pieces together; yes, Judith was right, they were all very close. "I'll have to be careful, and keep a low profile," she thought, which didn't really bother her because she had no intention of combining work with friendships anyway.

'Have you finished the filing already?' asked Pam.

Silvia nodded.

'OK, well, I'll show you how to print up the list for tomorrow's patients and you can get the files ready for tomorrow. If they haven't been here before, just create a new file, I'll show you where everything is.'

Pam went through the process of showing Silvia how to print the list, and how to create a new file, showing her where the stationery was kept.

It was a quiet afternoon, with no patients. Jim had consulted in the morning and in the afternoon he had theatre, so the clinic was only open for telephone enquiries and for catching up on paperwork.

At the end of the day, Silvia was glad to be going home. She enjoyed her first day at work but was tired. Whenever she started a new job, taking in all the information drained her. She was looking forward to going home and pouring a glass of wine and telling Nick all about her day.

Chapter 8

'Is this guy for real?' It was a Saturday morning shift and Silvia was on her own. She had just opened up the practice and took the phone off the answering machine when she received the call.

'Oh sweetie, it's Dave here, I need to book in with Claudia ASAP.'

'I have next Saturday morning available, does 11.30 suit?'

'Yes that's wonderful sweetie, if that's the earliest?'

'Let me take another look, just to double check,' Silvia ran through Claudia's appointment list again, but there were no other appointments available.

'I'm sorry, Dave, that's the earliest.'

'No problem sweetie, that's fab, book me in. So sweetie, I need 56 units. Please make sure Claudia has everything ready. I need 36 units in the forehead, and 10 around each eye, and oh I'm soooo excited, I'm going to look fabulous. I need to look 10 years younger, sweetie, for my boyfriend's 40th. I need to outshine if you know what I mean sweetie ha ha ha…. so you've got that? 36 in the forehead and 10 for the crow's feet, ha ha ha ha… So dear, that's 56 units altogether. Can you make sure Claudia knows exactly what I'm wanting, sweetie?'

Silvia thought he was having a lend of her but she acted professionally. Secretly she was wondering if Jim or Sally had asked a friend to call, just to see how she reacted.

'Yes Dave, I'll let Claudia know you're coming in next Saturday morning and I'll pass on all the details, I've booked you in for 11.30a.m.'

'Fabulous, that's great sweetie. Oh and I nearly forgot, my God how could I forget ha ha ha... I'll need some fillers in my lips too, sweetie. I need my lips to look just as fabulous as the rest of my face, so let Claudia know, won't you, dear.'

'No problem Dave, I will pass on everything you've said.'

'Cheerio sweetie, bye for now.'

From the telephone call, Silvia assumed that Claudia knew Dave but it turned out he had never met Claudia before. When he came in the following Saturday, he told her that he had heard good reports about her. After he had all the work done, the 56 units and lip fillers, he paid Claudia by cheque.

Because he was so flamboyant, Claudia believed him when he said he always paid his consultations by cheque. She had no clue that she would never hear from him again or recover the money he owed. The cheque bounced and the compulsory treatment form was filled in with a false name and address.

Chapter 9

Was that a whisper?

'... and now you begin to recall sensation ....'

Yes it was.

'..... by wriggling the fingers and the toes ...
wriggling and wriggling ...now raise your arms over the head
and stretch...... rolling over to one side stretching and then
over to the other side and stretch...... and when you're ready,
slowly sitting up.'

Silvia sat up begrudgingly.

'And then slowly standing..... Stretching up, raising your
arms above your head and ..... Namaste. Have a great week
and see you all next Friday morning.' Raja Dianasinghe placed
her hands in prayer position holding them between her
eyebrows and lowering them to her chest over her heart.

Silvia loved her yoga classes. She took up yoga after she
had her hysterectomy 20 years ago and she still enjoyed her
classes with Raja Dianasinghe. She loved the sound of her
soothing voice and her slight Indian accent.

Silvia observed over the years the changes in her body and her mind, that she was becoming more flexible. Previously, she had always tried to seek other people's approval and had set ideas about how life should be. But now she was more open to new ideas. In her search for fulfillment, to fill the gap of not being able to have children, she liked to read books on science, philosophy and the occult, her world was becoming richer and happier.

She had also taken up art classes with a lovely elderly lady that lived around the corner from her. Silvia met her on her way home after a long walk; she stopped to chat with the woman who was in her garden picking flowers. It was a spring morning, and the garden was in full bloom, with colourful roses and hydrangeas. The woman had on a large sun hat, with oversized sun glasses and was wearing an apron with a pretty sunflower print.

'What a gorgeous day to be gardening,' Silvia called out to her.

The women looked up and smiled at Silvia. She wore bright red lipstick and was wearing yellow gardening gloves that were streaked with dirt.

'Would you like some of these flowers, love?' the woman called out, straightening up slowly.

'Oh thank you, I would really appreciate that.'

'Betty is my name, love, come in,' she gestured to the gate. 'Follow me, love,' she turned and walked up the few stairs into her house holding the bunch of roses and hydrangeas. Silvia followed her inside and watched her rummage through the hallway cupboard, she found some twine and wrapped it around the stems of the roses, and then around the hydrangeas, making two separate bunches. She found some brown paper and wrapped up the two bunches to give to Silvia.

In no time, Silvia was sitting in Betty's kitchen having a cup of tea and talking about all kinds of things. Betty was so different from anyone Silvia had ever met; with evident pride, she showed Silvia her tea pot collection and her art room. She asked Silvia if she would like to join her art class, explaining that she held classes once a fortnight and that she had room for one more person.

Betty had travelled the world from Rome to Rio to Paris. She was an eccentric old lady, but she was so interesting and kind that Silvia agreed to join the class. There was something about Betty that drew Silvia towards her. Once she joined Betty's class, Silvia was hooked. She loved it and the group of women who attended were all interesting characters in their own different ways. Just being in their presence lifted Silvia's spirit.

Betty's house was an old cottage style dwelling, with beautiful glass and lead windows and creaking floor-boards. Her kitchen was filled with quirky teapots and knick-knacks, and after each art class she would make her students a cup of English tea with fresh tea leaves, using a different teapot each time. She would say they all needed to be used, and loved, or there was no point in having them. All the women would enjoy their tea, and now and again one of the women would bring a batch of scones with jam and cream for everyone to enjoy.

Betty was always beautifully dressed; she wore different coloured lipstick depending on the piece of jewellery she wore. Sometimes, it would be a vibrant red lipstick with a matching beaded necklace, or sometimes she would wear a more subtle colour, like soft pink with crystal earrings. It all depended on the weather. If it was cold she would be even brighter with her colours; if it was warm, she would soften them, she didn't want to compete with the weather, or try to outshine it, she wanted to embrace it and bring out the best of the day.

'You know, Silvia, before you do anything, take the time to beautify yourself, you must take pride in yourself, everything else can wait, your presence is needed for the day to take place,' was Betty's auspicious advice.

Silvia took her tip and put it into action. From then on, when she woke in the morning, she would always put in an effort and make herself look as good as she could. It became a habit, although sometimes she gave herself permission to be slack and not bother.

Silvia was younger than the other women in the class but she enjoyed being in their presence. They all seemed to have so much wisdom; there was never any nasty gossip. However, the things they blurted out would have everyone in stitches with laughter.

Silvia immersed herself into her passion of art and painting. She visited art exhibitions and museums, and read books on all different topics. She loved symbolism and the beautiful mandalas of Hinduism and Buddhism. She wanted to understand everything and took the time and care to research and contemplate. She found it fascinating to learn that the body held the universe within it. Art held secrets within as well, whether it be in paintings or poetry, and those searching would understand these secrets when they were ready.

She loved the quirky weird art of Salvador Dali and his crazy moustache. Georgia O'Keeffe's flowers that reminded Silvia of vaginas, and Frida Kahlo's raw emotional, yet colourful self-portraits that revealed the pain she endured throughout her life. She loved Leonardo da Vinci, not only for his paintings but also for his mind, his architecture, engineering and literature. She adored Gustav Klimt's colourful paintings, the obvious being The Kiss but there were so many from which to choose, The 3 Ages of Women was another, and Juliet Sira's dark mysterious paintings.

Over dinner she talked to Nick about all the things she was learning. While drinking wine, they talked about their day and enjoyed each other's company. Nick liked listening to her views on things and they always seemed to drink more than they intended. It would be at these times, when the alcohol had started to relax her, she would be tempted to bring up things that were best left unsaid. And so she wouldn't say them.

Each morning, Silvia woke up admonishing herself, saying things like, 'I'm not going to drink that much again or tonight I'll just drink sparkling water,' but by the time evening came, she enjoyed drinking those wines once more.

Nick wasn't into art and literature, but he did go to a few yoga classes with Silvia, and he did go to meditation classes for a while. But he didn't have the same passion; he was more interested in technology and computer science.

Chapter 10

Jim Istible had been scrubbed all morning. A few small biopsies followed by two large cases, one a breast augmentation and the other a breast reduction. He knew he was running over his allocated time in theatre but the next surgeon would just have to suck it up. He hadn't anticipated the extra bleeding in the last case. His team had to call in a vascular specialist to help assist, but by the time the surgeon arrived, the bleeding was under control.

He still wanted the vascular surgeon to examine the patient just to make sure that there was nothing untoward. When all seemed to be under control, he asked Katy to close up. She was actually more delicate with her stitching than he was. He was tired and just wanted to get home.

After leaving the theatre, he found the floor coordinator and asked him to apologise on his behalf to the surgeon he had delayed. Although everyone accepted that emergencies happen, the surgeons who were delayed were still pissed off. Having the morning theatre session's had its good and bad points, the bad being you were under pressure to finish on time.

'Could you find out which room my patient is in, I operated on her yesterday?' Jim asked the theatre receptionist.

The receptionist looked through the hospital list, 'You mean Shontelle Adams? She's in East Ward, bed 3.'

'Thanks,' Jim winked at her and walked off with his briefcase in hand.

'Hello lovely,' Jim said as he entered the room. Shontelle, a woman in her early thirties, looked up from her phone. Jim had heard her story many times before; she had two children and didn't intend to have any more. The breast feeding had left her boobs hanging and deflated and she just wanted to feel sexy again. She hadn't coped well with the first child. The way she explained it to him was having a baby sucking on her boobs had caused pain and stress and made her decide to bottle feed after two months. With her second child, she was a little more relaxed and breast fed for eleven months.

'Hi Jim,' Shontelle flicked off her Instagram.

'How are you feeling, lovely?' Jim was adept at the sweet talk.

'I think the pain killers you gave me must be pretty good, because I hardly feel any pain, just a bit of tightness around my boobs.'

'That's what I like to hear.' Jim nodded and smiled, 'Yes lovely, I've made sure that you're getting the best pain relief. The surgery went really well, with no complications and the result was amazing. In a couple of days, I'll take the bandages off and you can see for yourself.'

'Thank you Jim, I can't wait.' Shontelle squealed.

'For now, all you need is rest and remember no lifting. I'll see you in a couple of days.'

'Will do, I'm happy to rest and have some time to myself. I'm in no hurry to go home.'

'I can understand it. For most of my patients, being in hospital is like being on a holiday, a break from running around and coping with screaming kids.'

'You're absolutely right,' Shontelle grinned, 'Brett's carrying the load at home, with the kids and everything else. Do him good to experience what I do every day. As I told you, he wanted me to have the breast augmentation as much as I did.'

Jim gave her a wink and nodded in an understanding gesture, then turned to leave. 'I'll come by again tomorrow, to check in with you, bye lovely.'

Jim stopped by the clinic to do some dictation, and to catch up with Pam regarding a couple of accounts. Pam was sitting at her desk singing to Adele's song. 'We could have had it all… rolling in the deeeep…. you had my heart inside your hand … but you played it with a beating'. Pam turned to acknowledge Jim; she had noticed him through the corner of her eye.

'How was theatre this morning?' she asked.

'All ran pretty smoothly, although the last case proved a little more difficult with a bleeder. But we got it under control, all in all I'm happy with the outcome,' replied Jim.

Silvia was filing. She enjoyed listening to Pam's singing while she worked and, when Jim came in, she nodded a hello. She still hadn't felt comfortable with him as it had only been a couple of weeks since she had started working there. Was it his charisma? Silvia often found it hard to talk to men who she was attracted to. It wasn't as though she wanted to run off with him, but there was an attraction. She had been married for so long now, she loved Nick, but hey why couldn't she be attracted to another man? Nick probably found other women attractive.

By the time Jim was finished at the clinic, it was getting late. He decided to get some flowers for Sally who hadn't been feeling well for the last couple of days. He phoned her and asked if she wanted him to grab them some dinner on his way home; she was thankful for the offer saying she had no desire to cook. It had been a long day and Jim was looking forward to a hot shower and relaxing for the evening.

He rang through and ordered some Thai from a restaurant he and Sally often patronised.

'Hello, I'd like to order some food please. Yes for a pick up, under the name of Jim. I'll have two servings of Satay Chicken Skewers, one serving of Pad Thai and one serving of Tom Kha Kai and some plain rice. Thank you, OK yes, I'll be there in half an hour.' Jim hung up and headed to the local florist to buy some flowers for Sally, next door was a bottle shop where he bought some wine and straight to the restaurant to find the food being packed just as he arrived. Good timing.

When he arrived home, he set the paper bag with the food on the kitchen bench, and placed the bottle of wine in the fridge. He went upstairs to find Sally resting in bed.

'How are you feeling, lovely?' Jim handed her the beautiful arrangement of long-stemmed orange roses. He knew they would find favour, orange was her favourite colour.

'Oh they are beautiful, thank you,' she stretched up as he bent down and they kissed each other's lips, 'Mmm my hip is playing up again.'

'Have you got enough Valium to get you through the weekend? I'll write you another script just in case, and will prescribe some Panadeine Forte as well.'

'Thanks Jim, yeah I'm running out of both, this bloody hip, it makes me feel like an old woman.'

'Don't be silly, you know you're not old.' Jim gave her a reassuring smile and kissed her lips, this time a quick peck. She was going through her tablets at a fast rate. He knew she was becoming addicted; she was scared of running out of her medications, and became anxious when they ran low. He would keep check of her consumption rate.

'I know, I just feel frustrated today, the pain comes and goes, and I'm feeling a bit sorry for myself.'

Sally recently found out she had bursitis and tendonitis which were caused by the repetitive use of her legs when bike riding and jogging. She wanted to look good for her 50th birthday and had been overtraining in the last few months. She had been told by her GP to rest.

'Come on, lovely, get up. I'll have a quick shower and come downstairs. I've brought home your favourite bottle of Sauvignon Blanc.' He helped Sally out of bed and gave her a hug, kissing her forehead.

Sally had always loved Chardonnay until Chardonnay drinkers became a bit of a joke. Perhaps because of the Kath and Kim show, but, for whatever reason, she decided that Sauvignon Blanc sounded more sophisticated even though she didn't like the taste at first. It had begun to grow on her.

She went downstairs with the roses in her hand and put them down on the table. She found a vase and arranged them cutting the bottom of the steams and adding the sachet that came with them to the water. She stood back to admire their beauty. She set the table and opened the bottle of wine, pouring Jim and herself a glass. Taking a sip she sat down and waited for Jim. By the time he came down, she had finished her glass and poured herself a second.

Jim took the Thai food out of the packaging and checked it was still warm, before dishing it out between them. Over dinner, they talked about the practice and discussed the importance of keeping the patients happy.

He was such a smooth talker, all the women loved him. Even the men loved him. He had cultivated his charisma and had a way of flirting with everyone. He knew it was his charm that kept his patients happy. They needed to have their egos caressed. It was like an addiction for them, and by feeding their egos he knew his patients would keep coming back for more. He couldn't afford to have any negative feedback, in that way he was ruthless and would cut down anyone who questioned his abilities. One of his previous receptionists had remarked that some of the girls on whom he performed breast surgery were too young, and probably needed counselling rather than breast implants. Within a week, she was gone. He had made up an excuse that business had slowed and there wasn't enough work for her at the moment. Whether she knew it or not, she had doomed herself with her critical remark.

One of the secrets of his success was having a competent, dedicated team of people, and he wouldn't let anyone get in his way of building, and keeping his first-class reputation. As his wife, Sally had to look the part too; she had to look fabulous. They often discussed the importance of looking their best, toying with the idea of Sally having a facelift one day.

'Sally, I think it would be worth talking to Greg, his expertise in facelifts is second to none. It's best to have it done soon, so you have time to heal before your 50th. What do you think? You know you've been thinking about having one for a while now.'

'Yes I think the timing is right in every way. My jawline is not as firm. The last thing I want is to start looking like my mother.' She looked old before her time. 'As well, I don't have any commitments for the next couple of months. God knows, I need the rest with my hip. Plus I can work from home, now Pam is managing the practice; it's taken a lot of pressure off me.'

'That's settled then, I'll arrange for us to meet with Greg. Perhaps we can take him and his wife Linda out to dinner this Saturday evening?'

'Yeah, that sounds good,' Sally took another sip of her wine.

' I'll book us a table at the Conservatory on South Bank. Oh and Sal, I need to spend some time in Byron, you know I can't concentrate at home and I have to submit my papers by the end of the month. I've booked a flight for next Friday and I'll spend 3 nights there,' Jim said.

Jim wrote for a medical journal on various topics to do with plastic surgery, ranging from the instruments he preferred using, to the outcomes of different procedures, including case histories.

'That's fine hun, I'll contact Bella and make sure the house is in order,' Sally made a mental note to contact Bella. 'I'll probably catch up with some friends for dinner, and maybe see a movie.'

After dinner, Sally went back to bed. Her hip was really playing up, so Jim tucked her in with a couple of Valium which she swallowed with her last glass of wine. The best thing was for her to sleep away the pain. Jim went to his den, poured himself a glass of whisky and read for an hour or so before deciding to retire for the night. He went into the bedroom and heard Sally snoring, so decided to sleep in the spare room. He needed his sleep and he didn't want to wake Sally by nudging her to stop snoring.

Before he left for work, Jim scribbled a post-it note to remind Sally to phone Bella, he knew Sally often forgot things; she had good intentions but didn't always follow through.

****

Bella was employed to clean Jim and Sally's holiday home in Byron Bay. She was also employed to run errands and stock the pantry with fresh produce for when Jim or other guests arrived. Bella sourced the freshest fruits and local cheeses; she also made sure a full bottle of Jim's favourite Dalmore 12 Year Old Scotch Whisky was in his bar.

Knowing Jim would be arriving late that afternoon Bella arrived at the house at mid-day. She looked like a hippy. Her dreadlocks were tied up in a bun on top of her head with a coloured hair band. Her car was a beat up old VW, but it was reliable. She liked her job, cleaning holiday houses in Byron Bay, because most of the time no one was home, so that made it easy; dealing with people wasn't her thing.

After parking her car, she got out and walked up the few stairs and along the merbau decking, passing the concrete Balinese sculpture that stood between the window and the front door.

Bella stood at the door with her phone in her hand and checked her email again. She found the pin code Sally had emailed. Even though Bella was their regular cleaner, Sally always changed the pin code after each visit.

She walked in, opened the shutters and turned the fans onto low to air out the beach front home. She went into the kitchen and unpacked the produce she had bought that morning at the market. There was fresh fruit, some brie and blue cheese and a small jar of quince & pear paste which she put on a platter and left in the fridge. She left the crackers in their packaging on the bench next to the bottle of whisky.

After putting fresh sheets on the bed, she checked the ensuite to make sure it was clean. She removed a dead fly from the sink which she gave a quick wipe down.

Everything seemed clean enough. She dusted a few cobwebs out of the corners of the ceiling with a broom, and wiped away the insect poop in the corners of the floor. It was standard in holiday homes when no one was in them for a few weeks that they needed airing and the daddy long legs spiders thrived.

Taking a final look around, she noticed she hadn't opened the shutters in the back of the house which showed off the beautiful tropical garden and spa. After opening them, she looked around and imagined that she lived there. Why is it that some people have so much, and others struggle, she thought? She wasn't envious or jealous, she just wondered.

She grabbed her little pouch of tobacco from her bag, opened the sliding door and walked out onto the back decking. Hearing the sound of the ocean and the gentle crashing of the waves, she sat on the edge of the decking and rolled herself a smoke. She lit it and inhaled. She sat there feeling the warmth of the sun on her skin, a gentle breeze brushing a stray hair against her lips. Then she saw something moving under a bush, so she stood up and walked over to see what it was. An echidna was digging in the sand, its long beak of a nose poking into the earth, trying to collect ants.

'Hello little fella,' she said in a whisper. Mesmerized by the echidna, she watched it while she smoked. When she finished, she threw the butt down and stepped on it twisting it into the sand. She turned to leave before hesitating, kneeling down and picking up the butt. She couldn't bring herself to pollute such a beautiful place.

She walked back into the house, took one more look around, everything looked clean. She locked the doors, jumped into her VW, and drove off.

Chapter 11

During the flight Jim thought about how much he loved Sally. She was such a great businesswoman. If it hadn't been for her, he wouldn't have the success he now enjoyed. Because of her background as a practice manager, Sally knew all the ins and outs of the Medicare system and how to run a successful practice. She also introduced him to an excellent accountant.

Jim and Sally were a great team and he respected her immensely. He even bragged to colleagues about what a great businesswoman she was. They had enjoyed their catch up with Greg and Linda at the Conservatory and Sally's facelift was booked in. It had been a productive dinner.

He had three days to wind down. He loved that he could be away from the practice and Sally, and have some space and time for himself. They all knew not to disturb him when he was away in Byron. He had his papers to write, plus he worked hard and he needed the break.

It was only a two-hour flight from Melbourne to Ballina. The plane landed just after 5p.m and he caught a taxi to his holiday house which took about 40 minutes. Jim paid the taxi driver and thanked him; he was glad the driver hadn't talked too much, just a little small talk to begin with but he didn't go on and on. Jim didn't like chatting, preferring to look out of the window in a meditative state, watching the landscape and the change of environment compared to Melbourne.

He walked onto the front decking of his beloved tropical beach house. Standing there, he soaked up the warmth, it was so peaceful. He entered the pin code and the front door opened. Once inside, he placed his bags down on the wooden floor beside the antique statue of Medusa. The fans throughout the house were on low just as he liked them. The breeze was warm and tropical, coming through the slightly opened shutters. He had an hour or so to wind down before Bob arrived. Jim walked into the kitchen to see his favourite bottle of whiskey waiting for him. He grabbed a crystal tumbler threw in 3 ice cubes and poured himself a glass. He sat in his oversized brown leather chair.

He let the silence and natural beauty of the surroundings take possession. He could hear the birds chirping and the sound of the fans clicking. The air was fresh and clean and the view of the ocean was breathtaking. He loved the way the house was decorated with white walls and timber flooring, oversized cream couches in the living room, with his brown leather chair for contrast. Everything was minimal and spacious.

As Jim took his last gulp of Scotch, he felt the burning sensation run down his throat and into his stomach. The effects of the alcohol began to relax his body. He hadn't had a good fuck for a couple of weeks now, and he was getting horny just thinking about it.

He went into his bedroom and unpacked his overnight bag, then took a long cool shower, drying himself he walked into his wardrobe. Everything was perfectly arranged. He put on some cream coloured linen pants without any underwear and pulled on a black loose shirt. Sally had good taste. He admired the way she had decorated the bedroom, again minimal but sophisticated, with cream walls and a painting above the king size bed of a 12th century ceramic plate from Iberia. Within its pattern was a motif of a pair of birds in a tree, the colours of sand, gold and rust. The bed-head and bedside tables were contemporary, made of oak, and the quilt cover and pillows were plain cream.

A sandy gold coloured cushion matching the colours in the painting was placed on a chair to the side of the bed. On the bedside table was an earthenware vase with a scene from Majalis Al'Ushshaq (Assemblies of the Lovers). Jim opened the bedroom window a little, to let the breeze in and walked back into the kitchen.

Bob would be arriving soon; he poured a glass of Scotch for Bob and one more for himself, and then turned on his favourite music, Jocelyn Pook. He loved her exquisite body of work as a composer; along with her enchanting voice, he became engrossed with it. It was as though the music took over his body. He didn't have a favourite piece, all her work was delightful, King Charles 111 music from the play was one he listened to often, but this evening he was listening to Dionysus.

Jim was enjoying the music, when he heard Bob walk in and take the glass of Scotch waiting for him on the counter. Bob was in his early 40's and very good looking. He had tanned skin and a chiselled body with a strong jaw line and sandy coloured hair.

They looked at each, 'How have you been?' asked Bob.

'Overworked,' replied Jim.

Jim walked into the bedroom and Bob followed, as Jocelyn Pook played in the background, Oppenheimer from the album Deluge.

'God, I've been looking forward to this all week,' Jim said as Bob began to undo his pants. Jim bent him over the king-sized bed, and pulled his pants down, as he kneeled down to shove his tongue into Bob's ass and lick his cleanly waxed balls from behind. Jim's cock was rock hard, he slowly stood up and his pre cum was all that was needed to slide his cock into Bob's ass. Bob clenched a little but then wanked himself to ease the pain. 'God it feels so good,' Jim pumped hard, but then slowed down so as not to come too quickly.

The fan clicked and clicked with the eerie chants from the Deluge in the background. When Jim was about to explode he pulled out, Bob swung around to taste the thick hot cum pouring into his mouth and down his throat. It only took a few more tugs and Bob came too. They kissed and lay on the bed, relieved.

After showering and getting dressed, Bob went to pour himself a drink. 'Do you want another, before we go out for dinner?'

'Yeah pour me one, I'm happy to sit and relax for a bit, it's been a long day.' Jim sat down on his leather chair and watched Bob pour the drinks. 'So where are we going for dinner?'

'There's a new restaurant opened up, friends of mine have raved about. Thought we'd go there and check it out.' Bob handed Jim the glass of Scotch and sat opposite him, placing his feet on the table as he lounged back onto the sofa.

Chapter 12

Because Jim had taken a few days off work, Silvia was asked if she didn't mind taking the Monday off. It was part of her contract that, if the practice wasn't busy or if Jim was away on a conference, Silvia was required to take her annual leave or take time off by mutual consent. It didn't bother her because she was financially secure. They had already paid their house off, they had no children and it gave her extra time to pursue her art.

Silvia had begun painting a self-portrait. In the past she had painted flowers and landscapes, but now she wanted to paint a portrait and why not paint one of herself.

Silvia had set up an art room in a spare bedroom at the back of her house. The room had a window which looked out onto the garden she loved. There was a tree in front of the window which showed off each of the seasons. In winter it was bare, its branches looked like hands full of veins. In spring, small buds appeared and it would burst into life. In summer, it would show off with beautiful purple flowers dancing in the breeze. And in autumn, the wind would shake the tree, making its flowers and leaves wither and change from green and purple to yellow and brown.

It was quiet in her room and she liked to listen to nature through the open window. She could hear the birds, wind and rain and sometimes crickets. There was a large table in the centre of the room for her paints and easel, and, the walls held quirky religious artifacts and paintings.

Whilst in her art room she sat quietly and pondered. She wanted to capture the essence of her face. It made her feel uneasy, even sad, that the expressions of the people who came into the clinic for injectables and fillers had been erased. You could not tell their character; they had lost their identity. They all looked the same, expressionless.

To express one's self is the ultimate in uniqueness. Those who choose beauty through cosmetic surgery actually lost their ability to show the beauty of their emotions such as, joy, surprise, pain, loss and others, Silvia believed.

In her portrait, she wanted to capture her smile, which was not only in the mouth but also in the eyes and the whole of the face.

'A smile can even mask pain and hidden secrets,' she reflected. Her thoughts turned to the most famous smile in the art world, 'The Mona Lisa.' Was the Mona Lisa masking hidden secrets and pain?

The secret she and Nick held crept into her consciousness. A chill went through her shoulders and down her spine and she dismissed the thought as quickly as it came.

The phone rang; Silvia snapped out of her thoughts and brought her mind back to the present.

'Hello.'

'Hey Silvia, are you busy?' it was Rita. 'I just called on the off chance you might be free. How would you like to catch up for a coffee this afternoon, say around 2.30?'

'Sounds great, Rita. Actually, I have today off work and I was just painting, so yes, I'd love to see you.'

'Great, where would you like to meet?'

****

They caught up at a café in the quaint little town of
Beaconsfield. It was named The Corridor because it was
narrow and long like a corridor. They served good coffee and
great vegan and vegetarian food there. Silvia recommended the
new café as she had been there once before with Phoebe.

The best friends were chatting and laughing, enjoying the
friendly vibe, admiring the décor and reading the menu. They
were both deciding what to have when Silvia looked up to ask
Rita what she was going to order, 'Oh God, Rita, is that a
bruise on your cheek?'

Rita had a large bruise under her left eye which she had
tried to cover with make-up. Silvia looked at Rita's arms, both
of which were bruised as though she had been restrained.
'What the hell, did Frank do this to you?'

Rita's head sank to her chest as if to gather up her thoughts.
She inhaled deeply. 'It was probably my own fault, I asked him
too many questions about his past, and he just exploded. His
parents broke up when he was young, and I'm sure he's been
abused, maybe even sexually. He's had a hard upbringing,
Silvia, he finds it hard to deal with his emotions when he
drinks. He really is a good person and if he gets the help he
needs, everything will be OK.'

'What do you mean, Rita? You can't stay with someone who beats you! Because he was abused as a child doesn't mean he has the right to abuse you.' Silvia was seeing Rita differently. She thought Rita was smart and strong but now she was seeing a different person. A more needy person, someone she didn't understand.

Rita looked embarrassed as though she wanted to curl up under a rock and stop Silvia questioning her.

'He won't do it again, Silvia. The police were called by the neighbours. I had to make a statement and it's all on record. He knows if I go to the police he will go to jail.'

Silvia was seething, 'You know you're not going to tell the police anything. Especially knowing he will go to jail. What is it going to take Rita: you in hospital or even worse? You have to tell him to piss off.' She knew Rita would never call the police, knowing that Frank would go to jail. She would let that creep keep on beating her.

Rita sat quietly pondering, 'He did really scare me, I think he's suicidal, he said he would kill himself if we break up.'

'You know that's what abusive partners say. It's to make you feel guilty, like it's your fault. Please Rita, don't let him take over your better judgment. I've noticed a change in you, you're not as confident as you used to be. You used to love having dinner parties at your place and seeing your friends, now you don't have anyone around. It's not a healthy relationship for you. He's manipulating you and you think that somehow you can save him. People have to help themselves, Rita; they have to want to change.'

Frank's violent outbursts were increasing and he was becoming more dangerous. Rita knew it, but she pushed it out of her mind. Silvia didn't know the half of what was going on. Frank had punched holes in Rita's doors, and smashed some of Rita's ornaments against the walls. One thing Rita loved was decorating her home and Frank had begun not only to break her beautiful possessions but also to break her.

Rita explained why she hadn't seen Silvia for over a month. She had been trying to help Frank overcome his addictions to alcohol and marijuana. She convinced him to see a therapist, but he only did it because he was frightened she would leave him if he didn't make an effort. But it wasn't long before he was making excuses that the therapist didn't understand him and he was wasting his hard-earned money. He stopped attending the sessions. He preferred to spend money on Rita, he said, and bought her a beautiful water fountain for her garden.

After four or five days Frank was back to his abuse; slowly but surely he had isolated her from her friends and family. She didn't want anyone to see her bruises or the state of her house. She only kept in contact with Silvia because they were able to meet when Frank was at work, plus Silvia was Rita's one friend who she could trust. She knew Silvia wouldn't judge her like some of her other friends.

'I know I can't let him keep treating me like this, and I won't. Just trust me Silvia; I know what I'm doing.'

'I'm here for you if you need anything,' Silvia sighed 'let's order.'

Rita decided on a frittata with a side salad and Silvia on the spinach pie. Rita changed the subject by asking Silvia about her yoga teacher. She said she was thinking of going to a class one day to see if she liked it. Rita was more of a gym junkie and Silvia didn't really see her doing yoga which would be too slow and boring for her lively friend. She realised Rita was trying to keep Silvia happy by acting as if she was interested in yoga. Silvia gave her some encouragement. 'You should give it a go, you might like it. It helps with flexibility and clears the mind.' Her thoughts, however, were gloomy about Rita's situation.

After lunch, Silvia put her arms around Rita in a long hug. She did her best to look cheerful as she said goodbye, urging her friend, 'Remember to call me if you need anything, anything! Oh and by the way, if you want to join me for a yoga class, come with me this Friday.'

'Thanks Silvia, I'll let you know if I can make it.'

Chapter 13

'Now hold it for a little longer, five more breaths.'

Silvia hated the sitting spinal twist, what the hell was she doing here, torturing herself?

Raja Dianasinghe spoke gently and softly, 'Now slowly release the posture and come out. Relax. Relax. Now lay on your back, tuck your chin in so as to keep a straight spine, bring your arms out to the sides, palms facing up, release the lower back down and allow the feet to flop apart. Letting go. Letting go. Take a deep breath in through the nose and release through the mouth, ahhhhh, and again, ahhhh.'

Raja Dianasinghe went on to explain, sometimes you may not like a posture but you must breathe through it. Don't hold the breath, keep breathing, the posture can be uncomfortable and you may not like doing it but through the breath you can become comfortable. As in life things become difficult, and although we can't always run away from them, we breathe through situations, the moment will pass. We can find the comfort in the discomfort, in knowing that the moment will pass.

Silvia loved Raja Dianasinghe with her calming Indian accent and wisdom; mmm, this is why she came to her yoga classes, yes, this is why she was here.

'OK, now slowly roll over and sit up. We will be doing a seven minute chant. Sit with the spine comfortably erect, eyes closed with your face ever so slightly turned up, bringing your awareness and focus between the eyebrows.' Raja Dianasinghe spoke in soft tones like a mother whispering a lullaby, bringing a sense of calm. 'I will chant first round, then you all begin to chant after me, Brahma Nanda Swaroopa, Isha Jagadisha, Akhila Nanda Swaroopa, Isha Mahesha.'

She went on: 'Brahman means boundless or the ultimate reality. Ananda means the blissfulness or ecstasy of the Creator and Swaroopa is the form or image of the ecstasy of the Creator, Isha is that which rules and Jagadisha is the ruler of the existence. Akhila means everything, inclusiveness is Akhila and that which is everything, the image of that is Mahesha. So the Creator is referred to in so many ways, when we chant Brahma Nanda Swaroopa, we are saying everything is an image of the ecstasy of the creator.'

Silvia didn't understand what she was talking about but her dreamy voice took her to another place.

'This is a consecrated chant, which becomes like a coating, a shield around you, a cocoon of a certain energy. The intention is that a large part of you will become absolute stillness, but you will retain the liveliness of life around you. After chanting for seven minutes, there is a three minute silence,' said Raja Dianasinghe, quoting from Sahuguru.

Bliss........... for a moment at least.

****

Rita didn't get back to Silvia, but she wasn't surprised. She didn't think Rita was interested in coming to the class anyway. She was actually glad Rita hadn't come along because Silvia had her own group of friends there. They regularly caught up after class, and she didn't think Rita would fit in with them.

After the class, they meandered along the footpath to the café a few doors from the studio. Some of the women were really interesting and Silvia enjoyed their company. One of them was married to a barrister and even in her yoga clothes she always looked immaculate. Silvia was in awe of how great she looked. Her make-up was always applied perfectly and her figure was as perfect as her make-up.

Over coffee, they talked about the class. Apparently, Raja Dianasinghe used the Gita Yoga system. Silvia was puzzled at first because she hadn't been aware of any yoga systems. One of the women explained the sequence of postures that balanced the hormones and central nervous system and this was passed down through the Gita School of Yoga in Melbourne which was founded by Margrit Segesman in 1954.

After hearing this new information, Silvia decided in the future she would take mental notes of the classes and see if there was some kind of pattern to the postures. This was why Silvia enjoyed not only the yoga class but also meeting with the women afterwards.

Changing the subject, one of the other women in the group, also immaculately groomed, confided that her husband had been having an affair. Everyone stopped talking and listened intently. She went on to divulge that her husband had another woman living in their holiday house and he couldn't get rid of her. He had been forced to come clean and admit what was happening because the other woman wouldn't leave the house.

He told his wife he had taken her to their beach house a couple of times to play around. He didn't have any feelings for her, he explained, it was just sex. The woman admitted she was going through menopause and hadn't been interested in sex for a while. Anyway, this other women saw dollar signs and began bribing him, saying she would not only destroy his family but also his business if he didn't keep the money flowing. She started having cocaine parties at their beach house. Her husband was becoming more and more dishevelled. Finally he broke down and told her what was going on.

Everyone was gobsmacked; the group went silent for a good 30 seconds. Finally one of the women in the group broke the silence. 'Oh, you poor dear.'

****

Silvia was on her way to visit Phoebe, which she often did after her yoga class. She was still thinking about her friends and about what she had just heard. That poor lady and what a predicament her husband had landed himself into. Silvia was surprised at her openness and willingness to share such an intimate story. They were all such lovely ladies and so supportive of each other. She was thankful to have found this group of interesting women. She thought of her own situation and couldn't imagine confiding in the group.

Silvia decided to kill two birds with one stone and pop into the chemist. She could get Phoebe a little gift and grab some rosehip oil for herself. The chemist was overwhelming. It was one of those warehouse pharmacies that had everything in it. For a moment Silvia couldn't remember why she was even there. There were so many aisles. There were two aisles just for vitamins. Walking down one of them she saw vitamins for every age group and everything imaginable. And not just one kind of probiotic, there were about ten or twelve different ones. There were two aisles for hair care and soap and at least three aisles for women's makeup and skin care. My God, trying to find the rosehip oil was hard work.

Once she found the oil, she turned to the mums and bubs section. Mmm maybe Phoebe would like some stretch mark oil. Silvia couldn't make up her mind. She picked up a Moo Goo baby starter pack and decided it would do. She had heard good reports about the product, and was sure Phoebe would like it. She quickly made her way to the checkout, paid for the items and left, feeling a weight lift off her immediately as she walked out of the store.

In the past, Silvia had tried different vitamins and face creams but she came to the conclusion she was wasting her money most of the time. She finished up throwing at least half of the vitamins out because she would forget to take them and the expiry date would pass. It was the same with moisturisers, most of the time she didn't like their smell or texture. She had decided that vitamins and creams were just a ploy to take her money. It wasn't because she was tight with her money. If she wanted something, she would be happy to pay whatever the cost, but she didn't like waste. She made up her mind that all she needed for her skin was a little rosehip oil or coconut oil. As far as vitamins were concerned, less was best in her opinion.

Tall like her father, Phoebe had long wavy light brown hair with dark eyes, and tattoos all the way down one arm. One of the tattoos was a portrait of her mother and the others were memories of her childhood. She was quiet and shy, an introvert. Her mother's death took its toll on her, and when she broke up with her boyfriend she retreated into herself even more.

Silvia knocked on the door. She could hear Phoebe turn down the music and run to the door to unlock it.

'Hi Aunty Silv, come in. I was just listening to some music while cleaning, it gives me energy.' Phoebe laughed as she ushered Silvia in.

'I do the same, although I get distracted and start dancing instead of cleaning,' laughed Silvia. 'Here's a little gift for the bub,' she handed Phoebe the paper bag from the chemist, taking out the rosehip oil and putting it into her bag.

'Oh thank you Aunty, you shouldn't keep buying me things.' She looked in the bag and took out the Moo Goo pack, 'I've heard this is really good stuff, thanks Silv.'

'Yeah I heard that too. My goodness, you're glowing. I can't believe you're already six months pregnant. How have you been feeling?'

'I'm feeling great, Aunty Silv. The nursery is all set up; do you want to see it?' Phoebe had been getting the room ready for the past three months. Painting and decorating it had become a passion for Phoebe who had many people following her on Instagram. On her page, she showed her arts and crafts and the way she was transforming the room into a nursery. A lot of new mums were interested.

'Of course I do, I can't wait to see what you've been up to.'

They walked along a short corridor and into the nursery.

'Oh it's beautiful, Phoebe!' The room was painted a soft baby blue. Phoebe had painted a mural of a forest on one wall and there was a wooden cot with handmade stuffed toys around its edges. On another wall, there were photos of Phoebe and her mother, and a little book shelf with tiny children's books and little porcelain forest animals.

'He's going to be happy in here. I'm really proud of you Phoebe; you'll be a great mum.'

'I'm just so thrilled to be having a little baby boy, and Dad's been great, I'd be lost without him letting me live here. He's been so supportive; you know he's met a special lady and I really like her.'

Ted had always been supportive of his children. When he found out Phoebe was pregnant, he reassured her she could stay with him as long as she wanted. She had been living with her boyfriend for two years but when Phoebe told him she was having a baby, he said he wasn't ready to be a father. He wanted her to have an abortion but there was no way she could, so she left him and moved back in with her father. She reassured her ex-boyfriend that she wouldn't expect him to be part of the baby's life, but if he changed his mind, she wouldn't keep him from seeing the baby boy.

'Oh really, tell me more, he hasn't mentioned her to me, but then again Ted's always been private when it comes to his lady friends.'

'Yeah, but this one's different, she's really lovely. She teaches maths and science to primary school students. He was talking about having you and Nick over to meet her. Her name is Helena.'

'We'd love to come, tell him to give me a call when he gets a chance. Oh and by the way, have you heard from Jarrod? I've seen a few Facebook posts of him surfing and some great pictures of the places he's been to in Bali. It looks like he's living the dream life.'

'Yeah, he's having a ball; he's planning on travelling to Nepal next and hiking up to Machu Pichu, but promises to be back when little mister arrives,' Phoebe rubbed her belly.

They chatted while Phoebe made them a cup of percolated coffee and bought out some vegan cakes she made earlier that morning. Phoebe wasn't a vegan but she seemed to be heading that way, at least that's what her father thought. She became a vegetarian after watching an animal rights video. First, she tried to be a vegan but loved cheese too much and sometimes she gave in when she craved sardines, so technically she wasn't really even a vegetarian. Ted worried about her because he thought she wouldn't be getting enough nutrition if she went full vegan, but Phoebe assured him he was worrying about nothing.

'I'm having dinner with Charlotte tonight, and we might catch a movie as well.'

'Oh that will be nice, what movie are you thinking of seeing?' asked Silvia.

'I have no idea; I'll leave it up to Charlotte.'

After having the coffee and cake, Silvia gave Phoebe a big hug. 'That was delicious, thanks Phoebe, I'd better get going, Nick will be home soon, and I have to do a few things at home. Oh and tell Charlotte I'll catch up with her soon.'

'I will,' Phoebe walked Silvia to the door and waved goodbye.

Phoebe had always been a homebody and Silvia enjoyed dropping in to see her after her yoga class.

Chapter 14

Sally was still groggy; she raised her hands to her temples and felt the bandages. That's right, she remembered now, she was at home resting after the facelift. It had only been a week, she could feel the swelling in her chin, along with tightness throughout her face and neck, and some numbness in her cheeks. She felt a few lumps around her jaw-line but was reassured that these would subside. She was told to keep her head raised since the operation. Consequently, she had been struggling to sleep propped up with extra pillows. She would need to persist with it for another week, maybe two.

It was a relief the drainage tube was finally out. She felt so ugly with it hanging below her chin. It was gross. She could still taste and smell the blood. Her ears felt weird too because of all the swelling. Her emotions were all over the place. She appreciated being able to rest and recuperate in the comfort of her own home. While thankful for all the help from the nurses and Jim keeping her incision wounds clean, she was becoming bored and restless.

Facebook and Instagram were tiresome, it was as though reaching for her phone had become an obsession, only to look back and forth but see nothing which sparked her interest. I mean, how many times in ten minutes could Facebook or Instagram change? What new and interesting event could have happened within those minutes? How long could it hold her attention or distract her from her reality? She didn't want to know reality. Did she? Did she really want to delve deeply into her feelings?

The phone rang. Thank God, she reached for it without checking who it was, she was just thankful for the distraction. 'Hello, Sally speaking.'

'Hi lovely, how are you feeling, you old mole?' it was Pam, her best friend.

'How do you think I'm feeling? Like shit and I look like shit too.' Sally was feeling sorry for herself and her anxiety was building about the final outcome of her facelift. Would she be happy with it? The fear of aging was overwhelming. Especially since her hip was still playing up. It wasn't as bad as it had been but it still worried her.

'Ah don't be silly, you know you'll be looking like a million dollars in no time, and just think about how great you'll feel strutting your stuff looking so fresh and glamorous on your fiftieth. Keep your chin up, gorgeous.' Pam could always cheer Sally up; just hearing her voice made Sally feel better.

'I know, I know,' Sally replied and fired off a barrage of questions. 'How's everything going at the clinic? Is it running smoothly? How's Silvia fitting in?'

'Don't you worry yourself about things here, everything's hunky dory and Silv seems to be fitting in fine. Jim is a little concerned with Katy wanting time off, though; she's having a few marriage problems. I asked her if she needed someone to talk to or help in any way, but she said she couldn't bring herself to talk about it, not right now anyway.

So I just backed off, but Melissa told me she heard through some of the mums at school that Katy is having an affair with one of the dads. Apparently, they all do working bees at the school and have parent meetings, and that's how she met him.'

'Oh really, God, that's shocking, I thought Katy was happy in her marriage?'

'Well, who knows what's going on until we hear it from Katy? It could be the other way around for all we know and those gossips may have it wrong. Maybe Katy's husband is having an affair with one of the mums. Don't stress, lovely, we have everything under control. Judith said she could do more hours if needed. You just rest. I will pop in after work with a few bits and pieces to cheer you up.'

'Thank God, I can't wait to see you. I need some cheering up.'

'Bye, gorgeous.'

'Bye,' Sally hung up with a heavy sigh. 'God, what's Katy getting herself into?' She slowly rolled out of bed; her hip was not as painful today which was a relief. Hearing the news about Katy distracted her from her own feelings for a moment.

She walked over to her dressing table and looked at everything on it. Her jewellery box overflowed with jewellery Jim had bought her, and the fake jewellery that she liked to buy herself. She looked at the posy of flowers and her expensive perfumes, Hypnotic Poison, Christian Dior, Chanel No.5 and Versace. She reached out and picked up the photo of her and Jim on their wedding day. As she examined it, she remembered that day. For some reason, she did not feel beautiful; she was chubby and ugly. She was not enough. Why did Jim want to marry her? She felt privileged that he wanted her, but why? He was a surgeon with money and prestige and she was a nobody who came from a very ordinary family. Although he reassured her many times of his love, she could not shake her deep undercurrents of doubt and inadequacy.

She had such mixed emotions, sometimes she felt pissed off with him and held resentment within her, especially when everyone praised him so much. If it wasn't for her involvement, he wouldn't have been as successful. She was the brains behind the practice.

She slowly raised her head to look into the mirror, her face was puffy and the bruises looked worse than they actually felt, in fact there wasn't much pain at all. She looked into her eyes and could feel the tears welling up. It was as if she had been raped and abused by Greg and Jim. She recognised her feelings were silly. They hadn't forced her to have the surgery. She was the one who wanted it, but why couldn't she feel beautiful enough? Maybe after a few weeks, she would look so youthful that Jim wouldn't want anyone else? Maybe then his eyes wouldn't wander? Maybe he would only have eyes for her?

The buildup of tears could not be held back and rolled down her cheeks. The pressure that had accumulated in her chest and behind her eyes slowly dissipated as her tears flowed.

She felt a calm wash over her as she wiped her cheeks with a tissue. It would be good to see Pam.

She decided to take a long shower and put on some comfortable but classy track suit pants with a matching top from Country Road. She didn't want Pam to know that she had been in bed all day.

Sally was bought up in Frankston which had a pretty rough reputation for a long time. Her parents were still married but they were an embarrassment to Sally. Her father had worked as a labourer and her mother had stayed home to look after the kids. Sally had two older brothers and a younger sister. Her parents were big drinkers and would often argue and fight.

Her father had many affairs and her mother knew about them but couldn't afford to leave him. At the time, there wasn't much a woman could do if she wanted to leave. Most women of that generation put up with the abuse because they had no financial support, and it was easier to stay and complain than to leave and struggle. Her mother didn't take care of herself; she dressed in cheap clothes and was overweight.

Sally made a firm commitment to never become like her mother. While she didn't say it out loud, inwardly she knew it. Her life depended on making sure she had a good job and could take care of herself so that she wouldn't have to rely on anyone to take care of her.

Sally made sure she wore expensive clothes and bought designer brands whenever possible. The more expensive the better, like Gucci, Prada, Salvatore Ferragamo, Louie Vuitton, amongst others. By making these choices, she believed she would be OK and would escape her upbringing and better herself.

When she met Jim she was working as a medical receptionist and he dropped into the practice Sally was managing. Jim was very charismatic and was trying to build up his reputation as a plastic surgeon. He wanted to introduce himself to the GPs and had struck up a conversation with her about the ins and outs of the Medicare system and practice management.

Jim asked her if she would like to join him for dinner that very night. Sally was totally smitten to think that he would want to take her out. She had been divorced for two years and was just beginning to date again. She was married young at only nineteen to her high school sweetheart but it only lasted a couple of years.

She had a whirlwind relationship with Jim and before she knew it she and Jim were married with twins, a boy and a girl, Liam who was now living in the city, enjoying the life of a bachelor, and Chelsea who was living in London studying design and architecture. Together, they built up their practice and bought a house on acreage in Mt Eliza which was one suburb away from Frankston but worlds apart in class.

Sally had arrived into the upper class which is what she always wanted. A new consciousness came over Sally, one of being better, better than her past. By living in a better suburb, she was removed from her former self and elevated, not something she would ever admit to, but nevertheless, it was the truth.

Pam popped in to see Sally just as she had promised. She brought a bottle of Sav Blanc (Sally's favourite), a box of chocolates, and a beautiful silk scarf she had bought in a little boutique, plus a whole lot of gossip.

Pam really knew how to cheer Sally up, she was loud and fun and her laugh would make anyone happy. She joked about some of the women who came into the practice in the last couple of days. One of them wanted a boob job, but she smelt like a fart. They had to spray the whole place down as soon as she left. Another wanted lip fillers, but her lips were already so big they looked like they could suck an elephant's cock.

'Oh Pam, you make me laugh, I'm so lucky to have you as a friend.' Sally was in hysterics, then suddenly burst into tears.

'Sal why are you crying? Come here, lovely.' Pam pulled Sally close, and hugged her.

'I'm feeling sorry for myself,' Sally replied in between her sobs.

'You can talk to me, Sal, what's up?'

'I can't stop my mind from racing. I'm pissed off, everyone thinks Jim is God's gift. Everyone praises him as if he's some kind of hero. To be honest, Pam, he would be nothing without me. I'm the one who helped build the business and I'm the one who puts up with his womanising. I've told you about the rumours, about him flirting with the nurses.'

'Sally, you can't believe every rumour you hear. Those bitches would love to see you and Jim break up. You're overthinking Sal. We all know behind every successful man there is a super woman. Jim knows that too, he's always praising you.'

'I know he does, and you're right I shouldn't listen to the rumours, but something doesn't feel right, Pam.'

'What doesn't feel right Sal, do you think he has a mistress?'

'I don't know. He could be seeing someone when he goes to Byron. Maybe I'm being stupid?' Sally looked at Pam and burst out laughing, remembering Pam's description of the woman who wanted the lip fillers.

'Big enough to suck an elephant's cock, did you say, really?'

Pam burst out laughing. 'Yeah, they were.'

By the time Pam left, Sally felt recharged; there was nothing like having a good chat and belly laugh with her close friend.

'And don't you worry your pretty little head with the clinic, Judith said she'll take over until Katy comes back, and I'll keep you up to date with how Silvia is fitting in.'

'Thanks Pam.'

'Oh, and if you're worried about Jim having an affair, when he's in Byron, couldn't you ask your cleaner, what's her name? Is it Bella?'

'Yes Bella.'

'Ask her to pop in unexpectedly. You know, maybe get her to drop off a gift or something?'

'Don't know if that would work, but you've got me thinking.' Sally contemplated the idea.

Pam gave a cheeky smirk. 'Cheerio lovely.'

Chapter 15

Silvia prided herself on being slim and taking good care of herself although lately she noticed a bit of weight creeping on. Aging is not kind to women, she thought, as she drove into work that morning.

She was determined to accept the aging process, and not be like all those other women who couldn't accept change. In a way Silvia prided herself in being a little bit smarter than others, she wouldn't have to suffer like them with the fear of aging. Although since working at the clinic she had started to feel a little self-conscious about her weight and a few wrinkles which in the past hadn't bothered her.

Walking into the office Silvia overheard Pam talking to Melissa about Katy. They both turned to Silvia and happily included her in the conversation.

'Hi Silv, Melissa was just telling me about Katy, you know they go to the same parents' group,' Pam said as Melissa nodded. 'You tell the story, Melissa, you were there.'

Melissa took over, 'After last week's parents' group, one of the men stood up and said he'd been having an affair. He said he wanted to get it out into the open so that everyone heard it from him and not from gossips. He had asked his wife to forgive him and requested that everyone give them some space and respect their privacy.

Anyway, I overheard some of the women mention he was having an affair with Katy. I went up to Katy afterwards and she was mortified. She didn't think he was going to get up and tell everyone. She's devastated. Even though he didn't say who he was having the affair with, word gets around quickly.'

Pam butted in, 'Apparently, Katy wanted to end it and he got scared and thought she was going to tell his wife, so that's why he confessed.'

'Oh God' said Silvia, 'how embarrassing for her. What a prick for saying it in front of everyone and not letting Katy know beforehand.'

Melissa nodded, 'Katy is taking a couple of weeks off work to stay with her mother in the country to think things over.'

It was pretty much all they talked about at work that day.

'Silvia, it's not busy today; why don't you go and see if Claudia has time to give you a micro dermabrasion,' Pam suggested.

'Really, can I?'

'Of course. We all get them when we're not busy,' added Melissa.

Claudia's office was beautifully decorated with a white leather Zvago recliner in the centre of the room for clients to sit in luxurious ease as they had their treatments. There was a large rectangular mirror on one wall and an adjacent clear glass cabinet displaying their exclusive skin care range.

On the other side of the room was her desk, a simple but classy white and black marbled Vermont console table with a white classic executive chair. Everything in the room was of the highest quality, yet minimal; it was all about opulence and class. They were selling a product and that product consisted of sex, money and power.

Silvia was in the comfortable recliner while Claudia cleansed her face and dried it thoroughly.

Silvia heard the buzzing of the machine, and said, 'I'm a little scared.'

'It doesn't hurt, it just feels like a vacuum and like a very gentle scraping against your skin. Don't stress,' laughed Claudia.

When Claudia was finished with the micro dermabrasion she placed a face mask on Silvia and told her to relax for 20 minutes. She left the room after switching on some soft music and dimming the lights.

Silvia was in heaven, she had never had a facial before. She was thankful that during work hours she was able to have one. How lucky she was to have such a job. This beauty treatment was something they offered all the girls who worked for them, no doubt to make sure they looked their best. Of course, if they wanted Botox or any other procedure they would have to pay, but at a greatly discounted rate.

After about 15 minutes, Claudia returned and took off the face mask and began to massage Silvia's face, then she lathered on some fresh smelling cream and told Silvia to go look in the mirror.

Silvia's face was glowing with a bit of redness showing but other than that she loved the feeling of super-clean skin.

'Do you want a little make up on?' asked Claudia.

'Yes a little mascara and eyebrow pencil, please,' replied Silvia.

After applying the make-up, Claudia warned Silvia to stay out of the sun for a couple of days, or at least to wear sunscreen and a hat.

Once she returned to her desk, Silvia checked her emails and spotted an email from Jim.

****

To all Staff tomorrow we will be closing the clinic for a 2 hour lunch break to celebrate Judith's 60th birthday. There is a great restaurant within walking distance that Sally has booked for us.

Jim

****

Silvia was thrilled to be going out for lunch the next day; this job was getting better and better. And gosh Judith looked good for her age.

Pam called out to Silvia, 'Did you check your emails?'

'Yes I did, I'll make sure I forget my lunch tomorrow,' Silvia joked.

The next day, after consulting in the morning, they closed the office, putting a message on the answering machine and a sign on the door saying they would be back at 2.30p.m. They all walked to the restaurant that was only a block away. A long table in the middle of the restaurant was reserved for Judith. Jim sat at the head of the table and Judith in the middle, Pam and Melissa sat either side of her and Claudia sat next to Silvia opposite Judith.

Kerri-Anne and Sally arrived fifteen minutes later, Sally holding a big bunch of flowers and a beautifully wrapped gift. She handed them to Judith and gave her a kiss and a hug, 'This is from all of us.' Sally was wearing dark sunglasses, a hat and a scarf covering her neck. 'I'm not staying long, Judith, I couldn't miss your birthday celebration.'

Judith was blushing. 'Thank you everyone.' She opened the gift; it was a beautiful white gold necklace with a pendant circle of diamonds and earrings to match. 'They are beautiful, thank you.' With Melissa's assistance, she put them on.

Silvia hadn't been asked to contribute to the gift because she had only been there a few weeks; she felt a little awkward but just went with the flow.

A waitress came over with two bottles of champagne, and began to open the bottles and pour it into the glasses. A set menu of entrée-sized meals was being placed on the table. There were lamb crockets, spicy meat balls, quinoa salad with fennel and orange, arancini balls, tomato bruschetta and mini chicken parmas.

It was a lovely luncheon, and Silvia enjoyed watching the dynamics of the group. They were all friendly people although she did feel a little uncomfortable, unsure whether she fit in.

Chapter 16

The more Silvia delved into yoga and philosophy, the more she longed to be in touch with nature. She understood that everything holds within it a memory. She held a memory that she couldn't escape, a secret that she kept for Nick. She knew that life would bring this secret to light one day, but not today, today she only wanted to drink pleasantness and be one with nature.

Silvia filled her glass bottles with filtered water and placed them outside on her garden table, she said a blessing. 'Thank you water for nurturing me, I bless you as I know you will bless me.' She placed some flowers close by the water, lit some incense, and paused to listen to the birds singing. This was her drinking water for the day; she would leave it there for an hour or more so that the water could soak up the beauty surrounding it. She had read in Dr Masaru Emoto's water book that human consciousness has an effect on the molecular structure of water and that polluted water could be cleaned through prayer and positive visualisation. She would do her best to give it a go and bless her water. What harm could it do?

With knowledge came power and Silvia somehow knew, or sensed in a subtle way that, if she had a little bit more knowledge, she would always be ahead of the rest. Not that she admitted this inner knowledge to herself or to anyone else, but deep down it was as if she wanted others to look up to her, to think of her as special.

Her garden reflected her personality; it was overflowing without appearing to have any design or direction. It was beautiful like an enchanted forest; there were mirrors hidden behind plants and colourful little sculptures stood quietly next to shrubs. Nick had created three fish ponds. He loved the garden and took good care of it, weeding it every weekend, but it was Silvia who was quirky and found the little things that made it more interesting. There were secret places throughout the garden where you could sit and watch birds chirping, or just listen to the gentle whispers of the leaves in the breeze.

She sat quietly on the bench, watching the fish swimming in one of the ponds, bobbing up and down through the reeds. Sprinkling the fish food on the surface of the pond, she watched the fish swimming rapidly up through the reeds with their mouths opening. They gobbled up what they could and splashed back down, only to come up again for more. How many fish, she wondered, trying to count them as they dashed to and fro?

Hearing her phone ringing in the distance, she ran inside to answer it. Looking at the incoming call, she smiled, 'Hi Rita, how are you?'

'Hi Silvia, I've called to say I miss you, we need to catch up for coffee.'

'I was just thinking about you, we haven't seen each other for a few weeks. I was going to call you today.'

'Oh, great minds think alike,' she laughed. 'How about tomorrow morning? Maybe we could go to that great cafe we went to last time, what was it called?

'The Corridor?'

'That's the one,' Rita confirmed.

'OK, I'll meet you there, say 11 o'clock?

'Perfect,' replied Rita.

'I'm really looking forward to it.'

'Me too, I can't talk now but I'll fill you in tomorrow, bye for now, love you.'

'Love you too, Rita.' Mmm that was strange, she shrugged her shoulders. Rita had never told Silvia she loved her before, though it was a lovely gesture.

The next morning Silvia woke feeling happy to be on her own. She took her time getting ready. Nick was away in Germany for two weeks. He called her that morning; to tell her he had arrived safely and that his hotel was well appointed and comfortable. His colleagues were taking him out for breakfast the following morning, and he would call her again in the evening.

The morning passed quickly. After showering and doing some yoga stretches and a little meditation, it was 10.15a.m. She threw on some black jeans and an oversized light grey jumper. She tied her hair back and applied some mascara and a light pink lip gloss. Her skin still had a fresh glow from the micro dermabrasion. It would only take her 15 minutes or so to reach The Corridor from her house.

Silvia arrived at the restaurant five minutes early so she sat on one of the outside tables to wait for Rita. It was a cold morning but the sun was out and the air was crisp. It was relaxing to sit and watch the two young mums on the next table. Mums seemed to take care of themselves so much better these days, thought Silvia, compared to her mother's generation or even her own generation. One of the mums had a newborn who was asleep in a pram.

The baby was all rugged up and cosy with a fluffy pink blanket tucked neatly around it. Silvia could just see a tiny little nose poking out from underneath the blanket. The mother was dressed in dark leggings with tan coloured boots and a cream puffer jacket. She was wearing a cream beanie covering her silky blond hair; her eyelashes looked like two moths stuck to her blue eyes which lit up against the backdrop of her fake tanned skin.

The other mother had a toddler who was perhaps a year old, a little boy with chocolate smeared on his cheeks, sipping a bottle of milk while nodding off in a stroller beside her. She looked to be 4 or 5 months pregnant; she also had boots on but was wearing maternity jeans with a tight black and white striped top which accentuated her belly.

Silvia overheard them talking about trying to lose baby weight, a familiar sadness rushed through her as she thought of her own inability to have children. All the years she and Nick had tried to conceive, only to be disheartened each time her period was overdue but then arrived when she didn't want it to. She dismissed the thought, focussing on how lucky she was that Phoebe was having a baby soon.

Looking at her watch fifteen minutes had passed, she messaged Rita – Hi Rita, I'm here waiting, hope everything is OK?

Half an hour passed; Silvia wondered why Rita hadn't replied she was usually on time. She ordered a coffee and tried calling Rita – no answer. Sipping her coffee she checked her phone, nothing, no messages. The young mothers had left.

Maybe something had happened to Rita's mother. Rita had recently moved her mother into a nursing home, perhaps she had to go see her, she may have had a fall, old people seem to have lots of falls; or maybe her car broke down? She didn't want to go to Rita's house because Frank might be there. He had made Silvia feel uncomfortable and unwelcome in the past and there was no way she wanted to see him.

Before she left the café, Silvia gave the waitress a description of Rita and asked her if she saw Rita to tell her that she had been waiting for 45 minutes. The young woman must have picked up Silvia's worried expression as she too looked concerned.

There wasn't much Silvia could do, so she thought she would have a look on Facebook and Messenger to see if Rita had been active? She hadn't been since yesterday at 2p.m. She didn't want to intrude in Rita's affairs, so she tried to dismiss her concerns. Rita would tell her why she had stood her up when she was ready.

That night Silvia bought herself some Chinese takeaway for dinner and a bottle of Shiraz. She poured herself a glass and sat down to watch a couple of episodes of Grace & Frankie. The wine went down well and, as she poured herself another glass, the phone rang. It was Nick.

'Hi babe, how are you enjoying your time without me?'

'Ha ha, nice to hear your voice, honey, I'm missing you, but I'm also enjoying being on my own. I'm having a glass of Shiraz and watching a chick flick.'

'Sounds like fun, how was your catch up with Rita, you haven't seen her for a while?'

Oh yes, thought Silvia, 'Mmm, you reminded me, Rita didn't show up today, I tried messaging and calling but no answer. It's pretty rude of her, don't you think?'

'Yeah weird, maybe family stuff or maybe she was called into work? She'll call you when she can.'

'I suppose, but you'd think she could have let me know? How was your day anyway? Is it cold over there?'

'It's 6a.m. here, the weather's not too bad. I'm going to a seminar later today which is exciting but I'm sure you would be bored as hell.' Silvia's lack of interest in computers was mutually understood in their relationship. While Silvia acted as though she was interested, she was not a good actress.

'I'm sure I would, how are you getting along with your colleagues?'

'Yeah, they are easy-going and the food is pretty good, I like that these guys enjoy a beer at any time of day, even for breakfast. A few of them are taking me to a client's house for breakfast this morning so that will be interesting. You know the average Australian would think you were an alcoholic if you drank beer in the morning but here in Germany they think it's normal.'

'Well, enjoy your breakfast and beer while you can, there's no way you're doing that when you get home.' Silvia laughed, 'its 10p.m. here, I'll let you go, call me tomorrow won't you, love you'.

'I will, love you too, babe,' replied Nick.

Silvia hung up the phone and drank the last sip of wine from her glass, it would be alright to have one more glass; after all, they were only small glasses. Eventually, she noticed there was only one more glass left in the bottle, and she might as well finish it off.

She fell asleep on the couch, waking to the sound of her cat Molly scratching on it. Oh God, she dragged herself to bed and tossed and turned for about an hour, before falling into a restless sleep, and waking at 2.30a.m. Wide awake, she tossed and turned until about 4a.m, when she finally fell into a deep sleep.

In the morning, Silvia told herself she was never going to drink again but she knew, by the time evening came, she would enjoy that glass of red all over again.

She showered and went through a small round of yoga before getting ready to go to the Sunday market. After a morning of coffee, people watching and sifting through stalls looking for quirky art pieces, she spent the afternoon, pottering around at home before deciding to work on her portrait.

Silvia gazed into the mirror next to her half-finished canvas. Mesmerized by the colours in her eyes, it scared her to see her rawness. Studying them, she noticed that even though they were a pale green they also had slight specks of light brown with rays of yellow in them. Around the outer edges of her irises, there was also a darker rim of green. Her pupils looked particularly small.

In the mirror, she saw her mother's features. Could she also see her father, she wasn't sure? She began to think of her ancestors, her grandmother and great grandmother. They were a part of her; they were in her blood and in her bones. Within her, she held their strengths and their dreams as well as their weaknesses and vulnerabilities. Also within her, she held her father and grandfather, their struggles, their fears and their wisdom.

Her head was filled with the conversations with her grandmother. All the times she sat quietly listening to her. Her grandmother had a strong character and was ahead of her time in the struggle for women's rights, or her beliefs about them anyway. She used to say things like, "No, you never listen to a man." Silvia grinned as she remembered her grandmother's determined voice.

Her grandmother was a frustrated woman, having never fulfilled her dreams of being able to stand on her own without relying on a man for financial support. She loved her husband but resented not having financial independence. Silvia felt a fondness creep over her as she reflected on her forebears, the people who had made her. She could see her mother's jawline in her own. Life was a marvellous gift for which she was thankful for who she was. She could honestly say she loved herself, not in an egotistical way, not in a way that made her feel superior to anyone, but in a way of deep gratitude and reverence.

As she painted, Silvia was determined to capture her features along with the lines and wrinkles which showed her age and her beauty. She wanted to capture the essence of her soul, her heritage, her strengths and her fears.

Working for a plastic surgeon, Silvia had seen many people come in wanting all kinds of surgery. Perhaps because they didn't like their history and they were trying to escape their past? Perhaps because they wanted eternal youth and wanted to capture a time in their life when they felt strong? Or maybe they were trying to manipulate someone with their beauty? Or were they searching for some kind of escape from the reality of time? Silvia pondered these thoughts as she painted.

Whenever Silvia painted, time almost ceased to exist. She only noticed the day was giving way to night when she became fatigued. She started to pack up her paints and cleaned her brushes.

All of a sudden she felt a chill run through her body and her limbs began to trembled, she felt a sense of foreboding, something had spooked her. She slowly looked up at the window.

Startled, she sighed, 'Molly, you naughty girl, you scared me.'

Molly was sitting on the window sill, patiently waiting to come inside. Silvia opened the window, 'Come in.' Molly took her time, stretching first, and slowly crawling in.

'Hurry up Molly, it's cold.'

Once she was inside, Silvia quickly closed the window and pulled the curtain across. She went through the house to close the other curtains and made sure all the doors were locked.

The sky was grey and it had just started raining. She switched on the living room lamp and lit some incense and candles; she loved the atmosphere that the burning of candles created. It made the house seem more homely, especially now that winter was showing itself. With the heater on, the house was a sanctuary against the pelting rain.

She went into the bathroom and took a long hot shower; the hot water eased the pain she felt in her neck and shoulders. Whenever she spent a long time painting, her neck and shoulders ached, sometimes she would ask Nick to give her a massage. She put on her favourite pyjamas before going into the kitchen.

Molly sat on the kitchen bench watching her as she made herself a platter of cheeses, she added some of the home made jam, and fresh bread that she bought from the market that morning. She placed some olives and prosciutto onto the platter, and then poured herself a lovely glass of red.

Bringing the platter and the wine into the living room, she made herself comfortable and switched on the television. Flicking through Netflix, she found a movie that captured her interest, Under the Tuscan Sun with Diane Lane. What a cosy way to spend the evening, with Molly snuggled beside her, enjoying the movie and pondering the idea of travelling to Tuscany.

Chapter 17

After work on Monday, Silvia went over to Ted's. As Nick was away in Germany, Ted asked her to join him and Phoebe for dinner. It was playing on Silvia's mind that she still hadn't heard from Rita. Whilst Ted was preparing dinner, Silvia told him about Rita not turning up for their coffee catch-up and it was close to three days since she had spoken to her. Ted stopped chopping vegetables and listened.

'It's out of character for Rita to act this way. If you two had argued, I could understand her going silent on you. Let's take a drive over there and see what's going on.'

Dinner could wait, the roast still had an hour or so to cook and Phoebe would have it ready for them when they returned. They wouldn't be long.

Rita lived on a rural property close to Beaconsfield. As they drove up the long dirt road to the house, they could see Rita's car was parked in front. It was around 5.30p.m. in early June, it was the beginning of winter and the sun was just starting to go down. There was a slight chill in the air. It had been raining heavily the previous night and the ground gave off a sour smell of dampness and mud.

A dim light was shining from the window of the old wooden house. Feeling relieved Rita was home, Ted knocked loudly on the front door; no answer. An eerie silence hung over the place. The branches of a tree close to the house creaked in the wind. Silvia turned in the direction of the creaking tree. A raven was perched on one of the high branches and stared at her. She was taken aback but thought how beautiful it was. Ted knocked again, still no answer.

'Rita! Rita!' they called, before going around to the back of the house, maybe she was in the paddock checking on the horses. They couldn't see her anywhere. As they approached the back door of the house, they saw it was slightly ajar. Knocking again, Ted and Silvia called for Rita. Slowly pushing the door open, they walked into the house through the laundry and into the kitchen.

The house was silent; there was no background noise, no sounds from a television or radio. It looked as though Rita had been preparing dinner. There were potatoes peeled and a pot of water sitting on the stove, although the stove hadn't been lit. Everything was in order, nothing out of place. Her handbag was on the kitchen table with her keys and phone next to it. Silvia picked up the phone and saw the battery was flat.

Taking a closer look, they noticed that the potatoes looked grey, as though they had been peeled hours or even days before. There was some raw chicken on a plate that smelt bad and taking a closer look they could see maggots wriggling in it. A blue fly was buzzing in the corner.

Silvia had a sinking feeling of dread in her stomach. 'Something's definitely wrong, Ted,' and she started to shake. 'Something has happened to Rita, I know it.'

Thoughts flooded into her mind about their last meeting, their conversation about Frank and the bruises on Rita's face and arms. What had Rita said when she called? We need to talk, or was it I need to see you? Silvia's heart was pounding, her mind racing. They normally caught up on Fridays but Rita had called on the Friday wanting to see Silvia on the Saturday. Wasn't Frank home on Saturdays?

Ted thought the same, everything seemed in order but nothing added up. It was as though Rita had vanished into thin air. 'I'm calling the police,' said Ted.

Within half an hour, a police car, driven at speed, came up the driveway. Ted and Silvia were waiting for them on the front porch. It was getting darker and colder. Two officers exited the car and approached them.

'Hello, I'm Senior Constable Mike Davies, and this is Constable Rachel Singh.' Mike was a heavily-built man with a visible tattoo on his neck. His partner Rachel was well groomed, her dark hair pulled into a tight ponytail.

Ted got straight to the point. The fog from his breath was visible as he explained their concerns to the male and female officers. They all walked around to the back of the house, through the back door into the kitchen. The officers searched the entire house and found nothing out of the ordinary. Silvia told them about the bruises on Rita's face and her concerns about Frank.

'Wait here while I check the rest of the property,' The male officer instructed, pointing over to the large shed.

There was still some light left but as he walked towards the shed, the police officer flicked on his torch to see more clearly. He stepped through the large barn doors and shone his torch in each direction. The barn didn't have much in it apart from an old car full of dust which looked as if it hadn't been used for decades. He was about to leave, but changed his mind and decided to check the boot.

He tried to open it but it was jammed so he kicked it a few times, then he searched for something to help open it. Finding a large spanner, he wedged it into the lock and forced it open. There was nothing inside, except some old car parts. Then he shone his torch into the back seat and noticed a tarpaulin covering something.

He felt a tap on his shoulder. He jumped, and swung around, 'What the hell, Rach, next time call out, before you come up behind me!' he shouted.

'Sorry, Mike, have you found anything?'

'Not yet,' he opened the car door and with a slight tremble in his hand he pulled back the tarpaulin. More car parts.

They left the barn and continued to search the property.

Silvia remembered the well; she ran to the back door and yelled to the officers to look out for the well. Rita had warned Silvia in the past to walk carefully when going to look at the horses. Adjacent to the shed was a ground level water well. It was no longer in use but had not been filled in.

As Mike Davies approached the well, he saw a wheelbarrow next to it. It was tipped on its side with firewood surrounding it. He focused his torch towards it and down into the well. When he saw what was down there, he jumped back and gasped. Shocked and trembling, he called out. 'Here, I've…I've found her! In no time Rachel Singh was standing next to him. She peered into the well. Upon seeing Rita's lifeless body, she cried out, staggered to the side and vomited.

'What was he saying? Did he find Rita in the shed or…?' Silvia, agitated and confused, stared at her brother.

The officers came back into the kitchen, to tell them that they had found Rita, and they tried to break the news gently that she was deceased.

'I'm so sorry for your loss; it looks like your friend has had a terrible accident whilst bringing in firewood. The wheelbarrow was tipped on its side. It appears she has missed her footing and fallen into the well,' the male officer explained.

The female officer tried to comfort Silva as she sank to the floor, crying and screaming 'No, no, she can't be, no, no. I'm so sorry, Rita; please forgive me for not coming sooner.'

Silvia could hardly speak for crying. 'You went missing and I should have pursued it quicker. I might have saved you if I had done more to find you.' Silvia fell to her knees.

The female officer put her arm around Silvia's shoulder, saying there was nothing she could have done, nothing would have saved her.

'We will have to contact her family. Did she have any children, an ex-husband we can call or living parents?' Mike Davies asked Ted.

'Yes, she has a son and her parents are alive. I'm not sure about her ex-husband.'

Ted was talking to the officers at greater length while Silvia sat on the couch clasping a cup of tea someone had made for her. One of the officers perhaps? She couldn't think through all the grief and confusion. She heard them talking about Frank, that they would look into it further. Calls were made to the SES to assist in retrieving the body. They would have to wait until morning before it could be done safely.

Ted called Phoebe to tell her they wouldn't be home for dinner; he told her he'd explain why when he came home. He didn't want to tell Phoebe over the phone what had happened, knowing she was on her own. He wanted to hug her and hold her close. He also rang Helena and explained the situation, and asked if she would go over and stay with Phoebe until he and Silvia arrived home. He needed to be strong for Phoebe and Silvia, but deep within him a primordial instinct lurked and he wanted to punch a wall. He had to keep himself under control and not lose his head.

Phoebe sensed something terrible had happened, and appreciated Helena coming over to be with her. Ted and Silvia arrived home just after midnight. It wasn't a good way to be introduced to Helena, but Silvia took an instant liking to her. She seemed to be a sensible, kind and strong woman. They stayed up for hours talking, crying and hugging each other.

They went over and over it. Every possible scenario entered their minds and conversation. When did it happen? How long was she in the well? Did she drown in it? Would she have been knocked unconscious when she fell? Could she have been saved if found earlier? Did she die of hyperthermia? Did she suffer? Was it an accident or was she murdered? Why wasn't the well covered up? Did Frank do it? Where the hell was Frank anyway? Rita knew the well was there so why would she go near it? Was she drunk? She was making dinner and getting wood for the fire, had she been taking anything, pills or smoking a joint?

They were going around in circles trying to figure out what had happened. The police seemed sure it was a terrible accident. All they could do was wait until the police talked to Frank, and then for the coroner's report.

It was around 3a.m. when Ted said they had better get some rest. Phoebe was the first to give everyone a hug and say goodnight, she was exhausted and needed to sleep. Helena started clearing up the table; they had eaten very little; Helena packed the food into some containers and put them into the fridge for lunch the next day. She started to stack the dishwasher but Ted told her to leave the dishes until the morning. There was a half empty bottle of wine sitting on the table, normally they would have drunk a couple of bottles with such a delicious meal, but no one felt like drinking.

Helena said she had better go home but Ted had other ideas, 'I don't like the thought of you driving tired at this ungodly hour. Please stay.' Helena looked up at him with sleepy eyes, and gave a gentle nod.

'Good, that's settled,' Ted looked relieved.

Ted gave Silvia a hug. 'You better get some rest, sis, you can stay in the spare room. You'll find a new toothbrush in the bathroom drawer.'

'Thanks Ted,' Silvia dragged herself to the bathroom and opened the top drawer, there were a few toothbrushes in unopened boxes, she ripped one open and found the toothpaste. As she brushed her teeth, she looked at herself in the mirror. Her eyes were bloodshot, dark circles had appeared under them; it was as if she had aged ten years, overnight. Her face was puffy and she felt ugly. She spat out the toothpaste, rinsed her mouth a couple of times; she splashed some cold water onto her face and dried it.

She walked softly past Phoebe's room and went to the spare bedroom. It used to be Jarrod's room and still had telltale signs of him, like skateboard stickers on the chest of drawers. Silvia stripped her clothes off and threw them on the chair beside the bed; she couldn't sleep with clothes on. The fresh sheets were smooth against her skin and she was asleep within minutes.

Chapter 18

Silvia woke, at first she didn't know where she was. The night before wasn't a bad dream, it was real, her friend was dead. She felt a dark heaviness descend upon her. It took up all the space within her and her thoughts were muddled. She shook her head to try and clear it. She swung her legs and feet over the side of the bed.

Slipping on her clothes, she visited the bathroom first before going into the kitchen to make herself a cup of strong black tea. She was feeling a little sick and needed to fill the empty feeling in her stomach. Opening the pantry she found some bread and put it in the toaster while she searched for some jam.

Phoebe walked into the kitchen, her hair was in a messy bun on the top of her head, and her eyes were red and swollen. Her belly poked out through her half-closed dressing gown. The two women looked at each other with stricken eyes. They stepped forward and embraced.

Pulling back a little, through her tears, Silvia said, 'I'm making some toast, do you want some?'

'Yes please, Aunty.'

Phoebe plucked a tissue from her dressing gown and blew her nose. She started to make herself a percolated coffee, 'Do you want a coffee?'

'I'll finish my tea first and I'll have a coffee later. Where do you keep your jam, in the pantry or the fridge?'

Phoebe opened the fridge, 'Apricot or strawberry?'

'Apricot, please,' Silvia placed the toast on two plates.

Phoebe put the apricot jam on the table as well as some cheese and vegemite.

Silvia loaded her toast with apricot jam and drank her tea, while Phoebe spread butter on her toast with a thin layer of vegemite and added sliced cheese.

'I'm so thankful to be here with you, Phoebe.' Silvia didn't want to be on her own with Nick away, she needed to talk out her feelings.

'I'm glad you're here too, Aunty; Charlotte messaged me just before to say she's coming over this morning.'

While waiting for Charlotte to arrive, Silvia phoned the clinic. She decided to take the week off, so she called in sick telling them she had the flu. She had already decided not to tell anyone at work about what had happened. She preferred to grieve alone and with close family. She couldn't bring herself to go through the story all over again, explaining the details with her work colleagues. It was just too much to bear, and besides they wouldn't understand her emotions, they didn't even know Rita.

Charlotte took the day off work to be with her Aunt and sister Phoebe. She bought a variety of bite-sized cakes from her favourite bakery in Acland Street, St Kilda. Cakes always cheered people up. As she got closer to her father's house, she went to the drive-through coffee hub to pick up some coffees.

In a time like this, you could count on Charlotte. As the eldest child and losing her mother at an early age, Charlotte had had no choice but to grow up fast. She stepped up to help her father when her mother died. She mothered her brother and sister even though they were only a few years younger. Jarrod and Phoebe looked up to her and respected her for her strength and ambition.

Losing their mother to breast cancer was such a hard blow for them, but their mother showed great strength and courage; and they were able to say their goodbyes in the most loving way. She wasn't ripped away from them in an instant like losing a loved one in a car accident, or like Rita had.

Their mother had gone through a ten-year battle with breast cancer. It started when she found a lump in her left breast when Phoebe, her youngest child, was only 6 years of age. She had a mastectomy and had her lymph glands removed from under her left arm, followed by chemotherapy and six weeks of radiation. Silvia drove her to many of her appointments and was amazed at how upbeat and positive she was. All her hair fell out but she was proud of her wig which she said made her look rather sophisticated. She would parade around the living room showing it off to Silvia while Ted stood by adoring her.

There were some classes at the cancer centre which she was invited to attend. They covered the practical issues like managing hair and makeup. She eagerly embraced the learning and sharing with other women.

Slowly her hair began to grow again and she seemed fitter than ever. Five years later, a shock diagnosis: she had cancer behind her eyes, but once again she was winning the battle and it didn't affect her eyesight. A few years later, she found out she had spots on her liver and in her brain. She laughed it off with 'they're only spots,' and everyone thought she would just keep going. One day out of the blue, she visited Silvia and gave her a gift of some earrings Silvia had always admired.

Silvia hadn't realised at the time that her sister in law had come to say goodbye. In hindsight, Silvia was glad that she hadn't because it would have been too heart-wrenching to say goodbye. Two nights later, she passed away in her sleep.

At the time her children were teenagers; they had a loving family and didn't want to see their mother suffer any longer. They had faith in knowing that nothing could take away from the fact they had a beautiful mother, and she was deeply loved. It also left them knowing, in their hearts and heads, that each day is precious, to follow their dreams and not to waste their lives holding grudges.

Charlotte worked her way up in a large law firm to become the personal assistant to the CEO. She was very level-headed and prided herself on her organisational skills. Since she was a young child, she had kept a diary and wrote everything down, from what she was going to wear for the week, to the last penny she spent. It was her way of feeling she had control, and it helped her feel safe. She knew she had no control over life or death, but she could control everything else.

She was earning a good income and she and her boyfriend were able to buy a town house together. They had big dreams of one day renting out their town house and building the house of their dreams. Her boyfriend was a real estate agent; they had met each other through a mutual friend. They were a good match; both were ambitious, hardworking and loyal.

Charlotte burst through the door with coffee and cakes in hand; setting them aside, she raced over and hugged Silvia.

'How are you, Aunty?' She looked at Silvia with tears in her eyes. Charlotte was shocked when she heard that Rita had died, she had always liked Rita and felt so sorry for Silvia.

They held each other, sobbing, which started Phoebe off.

They spent the afternoon talking about the whole scenario, of what had happened to Rita. They talked about life; they talked about deep and meaningful things and about light-hearted funny things. They talked about their mother's death and about their father's strength. They talked about their love for each other and how they couldn't imagine life without each other although they knew that they could live without each other because they had experienced loss before and had to get on with life. When their mother died, it was hard on all of them. Their mother was like their best friend.

Charlotte reassured her aunt that it wasn't her fault. 'Aunt Silv, if one of my friends didn't turn up and I couldn't get hold of them, I would have done the same thing. I would have left and tried calling, and I would have waited to hear from them. Most people would have done the same, it wasn't your responsibility to take care of her.'

'But if only I had found out why she didn't meet me for coffee. If I had gone over to her house that day, maybe she would still have been alive?'

'No Aunty, there is no way. Do you know how cold it was that night? If she was cooking dinner, then it happened the night before you went to meet her. She would have been getting firewood for the night, if she didn't die straight away from the fall, then she would have died of hypothermia, and you can die from hypothermia in as little as fifteen minutes to an hour.'

'I suppose we may never know,' replied Silvia with a heavy sigh.

Phoebe chimed in, 'It's strange that Rita died in mysterious circumstances because I always thought that she was a little weird.'

'Yeah, she was, and it was her choice to live on the property, she knew the well was unsafe, and she should have taken measures to have it filled in, or covered at least,' replied Charlotte.

'And if it was murder, there's no way of knowing, it's up to the police to investigate,' Silvia said.

Spending this time with her nieces was a great comfort for Silvia, just talking and sharing stories helped ease her feelings of guilt and despair. She was thankful to be able to stay with Ted and Phoebe for a few days.

****

Ted arrived home from work that afternoon with a bag of groceries. He had decided to cook Kroppkakor, a favourite dish that he and Silvia loved when they were growing up in Sweden. He fondly remembered eating the potato dumplings stuffed with pork that his grandmother made for them every Sunday. They were good childhood memories, and tonight he wanted to share something good with Silvia and Phoebe and what better way than to share comfort food.

'Tonight I am making us some Kroppkakor,' Ted announced with a smile.

'If you can pull that off, I'll take my hat off to you, Ted,' replied Silvia.

'Well, get your hat ready,' laughed Ted as he laid out the ingredients, 'I'm going to take a quick shower and I'll be back to show you how it's done.'

While Ted was showering, Phoebe cleaned up the kitchen and set the table. Silvia changed into some comfy pyjamas that Phoebe had lent to her. She selected a bottle of wine from the rack, and poured herself a glass and set a glass aside for Ted.

'I know I shouldn't be drinking, but I wouldn't mind one,' Being pregnant, Phoebe knew she shouldn't have a drink, but with the stress of the past couple of days, she felt like a glass tonight.

'Sorry Phoebe, I didn't think to ask,' replied Silvia as she poured one for Phoebe. She didn't question her. Why would she want to make her feel guilty over one drink? In the past people drank and smoked while pregnant; there even were advertisements aimed at mothers to have a smoke to calm their nerves. Not that Silvia would encourage Phoebe to smoke or drink, but under the circumstances one glass of red wouldn't hurt.

Ted entered the kitchen and took full control, Silvia was very impressed, watching him kneading the dough for the dumplings and preparing the filling of pork and spices was comforting.

'Are you ready for a food coma?' Ted laughed.

'I am,' said Phoebe.

'So am I,' replied Silvia.

Chapter 19

Silvia was groggy when she stretched her arm out to feel for Nick; he wasn't next to her. She reached for her phone it was 2.22a.m. and naturally the house was dark. She turned her phone torch on, and used it to find her way. She could hear someone at the back of the house; she walked towards the sound, standing still for a moment. She thought she could hear someone digging. 'Nick,' she whispered, wondering where he was, she turned on the outside light and went to investigate.

Walking along the path towards the sound, she could hear crickets in the background. She stood there and looked up to see the moon light shining through the branches of the big eucalyptus tree standing proudly in her yard. There was a slight breeze whistling through its leaves. She turned back towards the sound that was coming from beneath the house. She knelt down and could see a dim light glimmering through the trap door. Standing there, she tried to make sense of what was going on. 'Nick' she whispered again, there was definitely someone under there digging. She opened the trap door.

'Nick, what are you doing?'

Nick turned to look at her. His face was that of a madman. He was trying to cover up something with dirt. An indescribable sensation overwhelmed her, a deep draining in the pit of her stomach, she felt herself sink and fall.

She woke in a state of terror, looked around her and sighed with relief. She was at Ted's house, it was just another one of her recurring nightmares. She had been having these dreams for many years, dreams that Nick was a serial killer and hiding bodies underneath their house.

She got up and put on the dressing gown that Phoebe had also lent her. Then she went to the bathroom and turned on the tap, splashing cold water onto her face. Looking up, she was startled to see Phoebe's reflection in the mirror.

'Are you alright, Aunty?'

Silvia reached for a towel and dried her face, 'Yes I'm fine, I'm sorry, did I wake you? I just had a bad dream, that's all.'

'It's OK, you didn't wake me, I was getting up to go to the toilet and get a glass of water, and I heard you in the bathroom.'

'Do you feel like a cup of tea?' Silvia asked 'I don't feel like sleeping.'

'Yes please, I've been tossing and turning and couldn't sleep, so a cup of chamomile tea is exactly what I need.'

They sat up talking until the early hours of the morning. Phoebe opened up about her fears of going through labour and how she worried sporadically about being a single parent. Silvia listened intently and reassured her that she had a network of people who loved her and would help her with the baby. They talked a little more about Rita and returned to bed.

When they finally woke up, it was already 11a.m. so they decided to have brunch at Rosie's, followed by a long walk around the lake. They were both contented to be in each other's company and for the sun to be shining on what would be another chilly winter's day.

Chapter 20

Nick was shocked and upset when Ted rang to give him the tragic news about Rita. His immediate reaction was to fly home to comfort Silvia but Ted insisted there was no need for him to rush home. There was nothing he could do to change what had already taken place. Silvia was staying with him and she was fine.

That night, as Nick tried to sleep, his thoughts slipped into the past as he was reminded of the pain he had caused another family. The anguish of not knowing what had happened to their son must have been excruciating.

Nick's mind took him back to the evening he was driving home from Sydney. He had spent two weeks there setting up a computer system for a new client. He loved his new job as a rep in computer sales, and the money was good. He had just married Silvia, his beautiful Swedish princess, and was looking forward to getting home.

He pulled into a service station to fill up and grab something to eat when his life took a turn that would haunt him for decades. As he was about to drive off, a guy tapped on his window. Nick pressed his driver's side window down to see a young man with curly brown hair and blue eyes holding a backpack. 'Excuse me; I overheard you saying to the attendant that you're driving to Melbourne, would you mind giving me a lift?' He spoke with a strong Irish accent.

Nick looked at him and thought why not, it would be good to have some company. This guy was of a similar age, 24 or maybe a couple of years older, and seemed to be an interesting character.

'No problem, jump in,' Nick offered.

'God bless you, my name's Sean.' Sean reached out to shake Nick's hand and threw his backpack onto the back seat. He was about to jump into the passenger seat when Nick remembered he had stacked a few client folders on the seat. The folder on top had the name NicksCS. Nick scooped them up and moved them out of the way on to the floor at the back.

'I'm Nick, I've been in Sydney for business.'

'Ah, I noticed the folder with your name it, what sort of business do you do?'

'I'm what you call a computer scientist. I set up computer systems for companies and fix any technical problems they have.'

'I know nothing about computers and couldn't imagine being tied down to a job.' Sean was obviously the chatty type and explained, 'Don't get me wrong, I'm not scared of work, but I want to see the world before I settle down.'

They talked about Sean's life back in Ireland and how he'd been travelling for the last six months. Throughout the conversation Nick started to wonder if Sean might be gay, it wasn't anything he said, it was his mannerisms. Nick didn't question him about his sexuality because at that time there were a lot of gay bashings and murders in Sydney, and AIDS hadn't made it any easier for anyone who was gay to come out. Nick thought it best to steer clear of talking about anything of that nature.

During their conversation, Sean pulled out a laminated card with a four leaf clover inside.

'Here, this is for you, to thank you for giving me a lift.' Sean handed the card to Nick.

Nick chuckled to himself; he took it and placed it into his shirt pocket, 'Thanks, mate. Hopefully it'll bring me good luck.'

'Aye, I'm sure it will,' said Sean.

Sean asked Nick if he had ever been to The Gap, apparently it was a well-known tourist destination with beautiful views of the ocean and was about 20 kilometres away. It faces the Tasman Sea and is located in the suburb of Watson's Bay, in Woollahra near South Head.

Nick hadn't been there before and thought it would be interesting to take a look. It was on their way and wouldn't take up too much time. It would be good to stretch his legs and do some of sightseeing.

Sean was a really cool guy and their conversation flowed well. Nick liked him and thought they could become good friends; they clicked like they had known each other for years.

It was summer and was about 8.30p.m. when they pulled into the car park at The Gap. The sun was starting to go down, it would probably be dark in half an hour or so. A car drove past them towards the exit and apart from that one vehicle there was no one else around. Nick parked the car, they got out and walked along the track towards the cliff's edge that met the vastness of the ocean. The sky was ablaze with the colours of burnt orange and red against the deep blue evening sky.

Nick stood there in awe, soaking up the fresh air and the view of the ocean. He was thinking about bringing Silvia here one day, it was so beautiful.

'It's breathtaking, isn't?'

'Aye it is' replied Sean as he moved closer to Nick who was standing near the cliff's edge. 'It reminds me of places in Ireland.'

'You must be missing home?'

At that moment, Sean stood in front of him and rubbed up against him as though he was making a pass. Nick was taken aback and instinctively pushed him away with full force. As if in slow motion, Sean slipped, off balance, grasping at thin air, he lost his footing and fell backwards. It was as though time stood still for a moment, their eyes meeting, both in shock, both knowing what had just happened, and what was about to happen, and then it was over. He had disappeared.

Nick tried to scream but it was more of a groan, immediately regretting his instinctive reaction. Holding his head with both hands, he cried out.

'Oh my God! What happened, what have I done?' He thumped his feet on the ground in impotent frustration. He stood there, his mind and body seized up, inert. In the eerie silence, he forced himself to step closer to the cliff's edge to see if he could see or do anything to help Sean. There were lots of shrubs clinging to the cliff face but no sign of Sean. The drop would have killed him.

Nick didn't know what to do, he called out to Sean but there was no answer.

'My God, what the hell happened?' Nick called out into the darkness.

He waited for a few more moments before he panicked, running back to the car. His body shaking, his throat and chest constricted, Nick gasped for breath. He hung on to the side of the car and tried to breathe normally. He steadied himself and went to open the car door. When he saw Sean's backpack on the back seat, he nearly vomited.

On the floor of the car was the picnic rug Silvia had bought in case they went for a picnic or to the beach. Nick threw it over the back pack. His hand was trembling so badly he fumbled when inserting the key into the ignition. Finally he managed it, the car started, and he drove away from the scene. Overhead, the seagulls flew above in circles against the red evening sky.

Driving home he ran the whole scenario over and over in his mind. Trembling with anxiety, he tried to calm himself down. It was an accident, it wasn't my fault. What the hell did he think he was doing? I should never have given him a lift. What was I thinking giving a perfect stranger a lift? He took deep breaths in and out, trying to focus. It was a long drive home but Nick wasn't driving the car, he was on auto pilot. His subconscious mind drove the car home for him, because he was somewhere else, somewhere he would rather not be.

Nick arrived home the next morning, having driven all night. He was weak and shaky as he stepped out of the car and hung on to the car door for support. He went into the house and into the kitchen, turned on the tap and drank two glasses of water. Silva would probably be home late.

He listened to the answering machine. She had called and left him a message. 'Hey honey, hope you had a good trip, I should be home around 7p.m. David has double and triple booked again. I've put the slow cooker on because I knew I'd be home late. Looking forward to seeing you, love you,' and she hung up. David was one of the eye specialists she worked for; whenever he was working, he would always be running late.

After hearing Silvia's message, he knew he had the whole day to himself. He walked into the bathroom and took off his clothes, placing them into the washing basket. He turned on the shower, if only water could wash away what had happened. If only it could wash away his memory. As the warm water splashed over his head and ran down his body, he was overcome with emotion.

He was angry and sad and began to cry, gritting his teeth as he punched the wall; his nose was dripping with sadness as were his eyes. The water was cleansing to his soul but he was crushed, falling on to his knees. Nothing could wash away the horror of the last 24 hours.

Nick decided to bury the backpack under the house, behind the wine cellar. It was the first place he thought of. Maybe it was out of some movie he'd seen. It was a stupid idea but it was as if his brain had shut down and he could not think straight.

When he and Silvia moved into their new home, Nick decided he wanted a wine cellar underneath the house. The house was built on stumps and there was enough room to manoeuvre himself in there and start digging. Each night after work, he would dig out a few buckets full of dirt which he used to create garden beds. He was proud of himself because the cellar had turned out really well. There was shelving and enough room to store camping gear and wine bottles.

When Silvia arrived home that evening, Nick hugged her tighter than usual and told her that he loved her. Silvia was overjoyed that he was back home. She picked up that he was a little edgy and emotional but put it down to some stress at his work and the long hours of travelling.

'Let's have some dinner, it's probably overcooked by now,' said Silvia.

'I'm not feeling hungry but I'll try eating a little. Actually I'm feeling sick,' Nick didn't need to pretend.

That's why he doesn't seem like his usual self, thought Silvia.

Nick ate less than half his meal, before leaving the table. He went into the kitchen and started cleaning the dishes.

'Are you OK?' Silvia walked into the kitchen and hugged him from behind as he was cleaning his plate. 'Don't worry; the dishes can wait until tomorrow.'

'I'm fine,' he said but he wasn't. His insides were churned up with remorse and guilt. Turning around, he dried his hands on a tea towel, 'Really I am, I'm exhausted from all the travelling, that's all.'

Silvia nodded, 'As I said the dishes can wait, I'm tired too; it was a big day at work. David shits me how he triple books his patients, it's so rude these doctors expect their patients to wait on them, but if a patient is late, they get annoyed. It's the reception staff who constantly have to deal with angry patients who abuse us. But when they are called in, they are polite and full of smiles for the God-like doctor.'

Nick took Silvia's face in his hands and pulled her toward him giving her a quick kiss on the lips. 'Let's have an early night, sounds like you've had a long day.'

After tidying up, Silvia brushed her teeth and got ready for bed. Nick was already in bed and Silvia snuggled into him and fell into a deep sleep. Knowing he was beside her made her feel safe. Nick fell into a restless sleep, tossing and turning throughout the night.

Early the next morning, Silvia was sorting through the pile of dirty washing. She liked to get it over and done with early so that she could enjoy the weekend. Putting the clothes into piles as her mother taught her to, whites, colours, towels, delicates and so on. She checked through all the pockets to make sure that there were no tissues, there was nothing worse than having tissues all over the clothes. She called out, 'Hey Nick, where did you get this card, it's pretty cool. Apparently four leaf clovers are hard to come by?' She was smiling as she walked into the kitchen holding up the card to show him.

Nick stared at her in horror, he felt a deep sinking in the pit of his stomach and his face was grey.

'What's wrong Nick, you look like you've seen a ghost?'

Nick fell to his knees and hugged Silvia's hips, his face against her and started sobbing like a child.

'What's wrong? Nick, you're scaring me?' Silvia felt a shudder go through her body.

His voice was muffled but she thought he said, 'I, I, I've done something terrible.'

Silvia didn't want to hear anymore, she wanted to run away, to pretend that she never found that card. She knew something was going to change her life. It was something terrible, had Nick been having an affair?

Nick poured out his heart to Silvia, telling her everything that had happened, he couldn't keep a secret from her. She listened to him and didn't say a word. Then she turned around and opened the bottle of wine that was sitting on the kitchen bench, the one they were going to have together that night, like they always did. They would enjoy a hearty meal, have a glass of wine, talk, make love and laugh, but not now, not at 9.30 in the morning. She grabbed a wine glass from the cupboard and poured herself a glass and drank it down. In stunned silence, she poured herself another and walked into the living room. She sank down upon the couch.

Silvia began to unwind as the wine kicked in. How wonderful the wine made her feel as its warmth flowed through her veins. The floodgates opened and she cried her heart out: she cried for Sean and for his family, she cried for Nick too, but mostly she cried for herself. Her world was falling apart, the world of romance and love, the world of families and happy ever afters. All her hopes and dreams had vanished in an instant.

After all the tears were drained from her eyes, and no emotion was left inside her, Silvia spoke, 'The back pack' she said, staring into nothingness as if she was in a trance.

Nick looked at Silvia with questioning eyes.

'The backpack, you'll have to get rid of it,' she told him. There was no way she could live there, knowing Sean's back pack was beneath her, hiding under her feet. She could not pretend it wasn't there. How could she entertain guests or see her family knowing a part of Sean was underneath their house?

'Where, what do you mean?' asked Nick.

'I don't care, just get rid of it, it can't stay under our house. You'll have to dig it up and throw it in the bin or better still burn it.'

Nick kneeled before Silvia and embraced her tenderly. 'We will get through this.'

Nick dug it up and placed it in the garbage bin. They decided that garbage dumps hold so much rubbish that nothing would be found there, and even if it was, no one would ever know they had put it there. Nick had looked through the bag. There was nothing in it apart from clothes. Sean must have had his passport and wallet on him when he went over the cliff.

For the next few weeks and months they followed the news intently, and heard nothing about Sean. His body was never found, and no one ever reported him missing. There were reports of gay bashings, and even murders, but nothing about Sean. Silvia and Nick never spoke of it again but it lay silently between them. For her part, Silvia formed the belief that she and Nick couldn't have children as a punishment for their crime, the crime of never coming forward, for being young and selfish and wanting to carry on with their lives as though nothing had happened.

Nick could never free his mind from what happened at the Gap. Even though he never spoke of it again to Silvia, he researched the history and became fascinated with the area which was the site of a shipwreck which caused the loss of 121 lives in 1857. The Gap also became infamous for the number of suicides. It was a place filled with ghosts. Now, an Irish backpacker named Sean was one of those ghosts. Only no one else knew about him which haunted Nick whose conscience was stricken with guilt.

****

Nick fell into a restless sleep as his mind wandered from Rita to Sean and back again. Was karma coming around, and playing its part? Not knowing what happened to Rita was heart wrenching, yet Sean's family would have been suffering the same torment for the past 20 years. Nick struggled to fall asleep, his heart was with Silvia, he wanted to be with her but he had four more nights in Germany.

Chapter 21

After spending two nights with Ted and Phoebe, Silvia wanted to have some time alone. She also needed to get home to feed Molly. Ted had insisted she stay with them until Nick returned home, but Silvia convinced him she needed some space.

Silvia had become accustomed to being alone when Nick was away for work. She had always been able to occupy herself with art projects or reading. She liked the peacefulness of a quiet home.

'Oh, why did she casually throw the remote control into her handbag?' When she reached the driveway, she had to waste time fishing around in her bag for it. It was strange that when she married Nick they were the first people they knew to join a video library. They thought it was amazing to be able to choose whatever movie you wanted, take it home and watch it on your own television. Yet here she was opening her garage door with a remote control. She couldn't understand how it worked but she was using it. Technology had made huge advances and a remote control was nothing compared to what was being achieved now. Finally she found it!

Once the car was in the garage, she pressed the remote again and the door closed behind her. As she left the car, she could hear Molly meowing inside the house; poor Molly must be starving. She opened the door and Molly started rubbing her face up against Silvia's leg. 'You must be hungry Molly, here let me get you some fresh water and food.' She washed Molly's dish and filled it with her dry biscuits while Molly was head butting her arm. Silvia felt guilty for leaving her. She began to cry, her emotions were a mess. She sat on the floor of the laundry letting her emotions take over while Molly chewed her food, oblivious to her owner's melancholy.

After about 10 minutes, Silvia picked herself up and decided to have a shower. She changed her clothes, choosing black leggings with a black merino sweater. Did she choose black because of the way she was feeling? Subconsciously, probably yes. The shower made her feel a little better but the quietness of the house was surprisingly unbearable. She decided to go for a walk.

The sun was shining but the air was cold, Silvia rugged up before she went out, donning her beanie and wrapping a blue knitted scarf around her neck. Her body felt warm but her hands and face were exposed to the bitter cold. Breathing in deeply, she tried to shake off the cloud of despair hanging over her.

Silvia walked down a couple of streets and through the local park. It was quiet, the only other person was an elderly man walking his dog in the distance. She listened to the wind rustling through the leaves of the large eucalyptus trees lining both sides of the path. Looking up, she could see birds fluttering amongst the branches. A tall ghost gum stood like a majestic sentinel a couple of metres off the track. As she walked by the lemon myrtle tree, she stopped to pick some of its leaves. Squeezing them between her fingers, she brought them to her nose to breath in the tangy aroma. She could hear the screeching cockatoos as they flew past her, some were white and yellow but a few had pink and red patches.

She headed towards the man-made lake in the middle of the park. She sat down on one of the seats overlooking the lake and watched the ducks. It was a peaceful scene and she tried to take in its beauty. She wanted to just be, like all the gurus suggest, to be in the moment. Some of the ducks were flying in and landing with trails of water splashing behind, others had ducklings proudly following along, but they couldn't hold her attention for long. She couldn't stand the quietness, so she followed the path back and walked along the street.

When she reached the familiar house, she knocked on the door; she could hear Betty fumbling to open it. There was something about Betty that made Silvia feel safe, perhaps she was the mother that Silvia never had. She was wise and kind, not like Silvia's mother who was always judgmental and negative. Or maybe to some people Silvia's mother was wise and kind and Silvia just couldn't see it? Perhaps that's how things are: sometimes you need someone who's not too close to hear your deepest thoughts and worries, and Betty filled that role perfectly for Silvia.

'Hello love, how are you?' Betty was wearing a green dress with bright pink lipstick. Her hair was swirled into a neat bun, and she was wearing an art smock to cover her dress.

'I'm sorry Betty, I hope I haven't interrupted you,' she apologised and burst into tears.

'Oh love, no, of course you haven't. Come in and have a cup of tea.' Betty opened her arms and ushered her in, sitting her down at the kitchen table. Taking off her smock, she washed her hands and prepared the teapot with fresh tea leaves.

Silvia poured her heart out to Betty while Betty poured her a cup of tea. She listened intently to everything Silvia had to say, including about Sean and Rita. Betty patted Silvia's arm and nodded as Silvia spoke. She didn't judge her or advise her to do anything; she just listened and allowed Silvia the space she needed to purge everything she was holding onto.

Betty placed a box of tissues beside Silvia as she continued her story. Silvia paused, to say thank you as she wiped away her tears and blew her nose.

Silvia felt relieved after she had blurted everything out, she felt safe around Betty and she was glad for her company, but then doubt crept in and she wondered if she had done the right thing. Should she have told her about Sean, she wasn't sure, but the weight had lifted off her for the moment?

Betty reassured her that everything would be OK and that life has mysterious ways of sorting things out.

****

After Silvia left, Betty returned to her art room, putting her smock back on, she took a deep breath in and exhaled as she resumed painting. On the canvas was a scene of purple lilies against a backdrop of white snow and a deep blue sky, she hummed to the tune of Que Sera, Sera.

Chapter 22

The sky was grey and the wind blew cold, the perfect setting for a day of mourning. Nick's strong arm held Silvia close to him as they both stood beside the gravesite. Dirt was piled up beside the deep hole in which Rita's remains would rest. There were about 40 to 50 people gathered around, Rita's mother was sitting in a wheel chair seemingly oblivious to what was happening, her father stood strong waiting for the scheduled service to begin.

It had been two weeks since Rita's body was retrieved. The coroner had not released the body until the police had collected all the evidence. Rita's father began to speak, announcing it could take months until they found out the actual cause of her death. He concluded they may never know the exact circumstances of how and why she had fallen into the well.

Silvia listened earnestly; she could feel the cold of the damp earth coming through her shoes. She wore boots with thin stockings, a black winter dress and a dark woollen jacket. In hindsight, she should have worn thick socks. She was thankful she had Nick so close beside her; together they could keep each other warm.

Her mind kept bringing her back over and over again to Rita, her dear sweet funny friend. How would she have felt in that cold and dark well, wet and muddy she wouldn't have lasted long? If she hadn't drowned she would have died of hypothermia? Her body was found after she had been lying there for days, was she curled up in a foetal position, was her skin swollen with water, and was she unrecognizable? Silvia wondered. Her body had been retrieved, pulled out of the earth only to be put back in, but now she was packaged up neatly in a coffin.

Silvia searched through the faces to see if Frank was there but she couldn't see him, or could she? There was a dark shadow beside a tree in the background. She attempted to focus on him but couldn't see clearly through the crowd. If it was him, he didn't stay around for long.

The priest gave a small sermon, blessing Rita's body and quoting scripture. In a monotone voice he read from Ecclesiastes 3: 1-4 'There is a time for everything, a time to be born and a time to die, a time to plant and a time to uproot, a time to kill and a time to heal, a time to tear down and a time to build, a time to weep and a time to laugh, a time to mourn and a time to dance.'

And then he read from Romans 8: 38-39, 'For I am convinced that neither death nor life, neither angels nor demons, neither the present nor the future, nor any powers, neither height nor depth, nor anything else in all creation, will be able to separate us from God's love.' He reassured everyone that Rita was in the hands of God and she would be taken care of, lovingly.

Requesting everyone to join him in the Lords' prayer, the priest began with, 'Our father who art in heaven,' and the mourners joined in, 'Hallowed be thy name; thy kingdom come; thy will be done on earth as it is in heaven. Give us this day our daily bread; and forgive us our trespasses as we forgive those who trespass against us; and lead us not into temptation, but deliver us from evil. Amen.'

Standing aside he asked the mourners to show their respects by placing a flower onto the coffin. Slowly and respectfully, one by one, they came forward, some had their own posies, others took a rose from the priest; it was muddy so everyone tread carefully so as not to slip. Nick held Silvia's hand as she stepped in to take a rose from the priest; she passed one to Nick and took another for herself; they lent in and threw them onto the casket at the same time.

Once all the flowers had covered the coffin, everyone stood back while the straps holding it steady were released and gently the coffin lowered. Overhead an eagle flew by and the sounds of weeping could not be contained.

Once the weeping subsided, her father spoke again asking all close friends and family to join them for a light supper at the local community centre.

Silvia and Nick made their way to the car, 'I think I saw Frank in the background standing next to a tree, did you see him?' asked Silvia.

'No, I didn't, I wonder if he will be at the community centre, I'd like to know what he has to say.' Nick had met Frank on a number of occasions; he didn't really have much in common with him but had tried to get to know him. The first time was when Rita invited them over for dinner, but when they arrived, Frank was nowhere to be seen. Rita made excuses for him saying he was just taking a nap because he had a hard day at work. When Frank finally showed his face, he was drunk and he didn't sit with them while they ate but stood behind Rita talking nonstop about his work.

It was an uncomfortable night and they left early. The next time Nick met him was when he bumped into him and Rita at the shopping centre, Frank had his arm resting on her shoulders around her neck. He pulled her closer to him when he saw Nick, giving a sign to say he owned her and, once again, Frank only talked about himself.

Her grief, anger and frustration boiled over and Silvia did not hold back, 'I doubt he will be there, he's a lowlife piece of shit, Nick, I told you she had bruises on her face and arms that time I caught up with her for lunch.'

'Silvia, you can't assume he killed her just because of some bruises. You don't know what goes on in people's lives. He's probably grieving like everybody else is.' Nick tried to give him the benefit of the doubt, but wasn't too sure if he deserved it.

'I've never liked him, there's just something about him I don't trust.'

'Let's just show our respects and hear what her family has to say.'

Nick searched Google maps for the address of the community centre, it was a short 10 minute drive from the cemetery. They drove in silence, both taking in the view of the hills and countryside. The peacefulness of the scenery calmed Silvia's mind. There was something about the rolling hills and green grass that took her to another place deep within, that made her feel everything would be OK.

In the distance coming up on the right was a wooden churchlike building, the community centre.

'This must be it.' Nick indicated and turned onto the long dirt driveway.

A lot of people had already arrived. After parking the car, Nick and Silvia sat and watched, they didn't want to rush in because they wanted the family to gather first. They saw Rita's son who was in his late twenties. He was walking with his girlfriend and it had to be his father, Rita's ex-husband. Once they entered the community centre, Nick took Silvia by the hand, 'Come on, let's go in.'

It was warm inside and had a good community atmosphere. There were sandwiches and cups of tea and coffee placed neatly on a large table in the centre of the room, with seats placed along the walls. People were chatting away as they helped themselves to the food and beverages.

Silvia was interested to hear people talking about her friend. Rita had other friends from the gym and her work. They cared about Rita as much as she did. They had all lost a dear friend like she had. She overheard a group of women questioning the strange way in which Rita died; obviously they had the same doubts and suspicions as she. With so many unanswered questions, everyone tried to fill in the gaps with their own ideas.

Nick handed Silvia a cup of coffee and a plate of sandwiches, they then found a nearby seat and tried to figure out who everyone was. 'I think that might be her Aunty because she looks like her mother?' said Silvia.

'I think you're right, she does look like her, she must be her mother's younger sister. Does Rita's mum have dementia?' Nick queried.

Rita's mum was sitting in the wheelchair, her eyes glazed, staring blankly ahead. The woman Silvia assumed was her sister was handing her a cup of tea.

'No, I don't think so, Rita never mentioned it to me, she might appear vague because she's distressed.'

'I can't see Frank anywhere.'

'That's because he's a spineless bastard.' Silvia said under her breath.

Rita's father asked everyone to fill their plates and take a seat; he was going to give a speech. Once everyone had taken a seat and were quiet, her father began to give an overview of Rita's life. He told stories of their life in Russia and how Rita had travelled the world as a teenager with her cousin. He spoke about her love for literature and her travels to some of the most beautiful libraries in Europe. She was interested in Johannes Gutenberg who introduced printing to Europe and travelled extensively through Germany.

He spoke about Rita's heartbreak when her boyfriend of five years died trying to save his best friend from drowning. They had been fishing when their tinny boat was tipped over by a freak wave; the friend survived and told the story of how Rita's boyfriend was already near the shore when he saw his friend struggling. He came back to help him telling him to hold onto the tinny while he swam back to shore to get help. He reached the shore and managed to alert someone but, died of a heart attack brought on by exhaustion.

Silvia was fascinated to hear these stories about Rita because Rita had never spoken to her about her past.

Silvia and Rita had been friends for about 10 years, having met at the local library. Silvia was researching art and Rita was browsing the shelves when they bumped into each other. Rita was so easy to talk to that Silvia took an instant liking to her. Rita asked Silvia if she had been to the new café that had opened up next door to the library. Silvia said she hadn't, so she asked Rita to join her for brunch, and from that day they became good friends.

For Silvia, it was healing to spend that afternoon celebrating Rita's life, and to hear about what she had done and achieved, rather than to dwell on her tragic death.

After the funeral they returned home and Silvia locked herself in her room. Resentment had been building up for years and the stress of the funeral was a tipping point. Silvia was about to explode.

Nick knocked on the door. 'Are you OK?'

'What do you think?' she hissed.

'Open the door.'

She opened the door, turned around and sat on the bed. Nick sat next to her, putting his arm around her shoulder. Silvia shrugged his arm away.

'What's wrong, honey?'

'I'm sick of keeping my mouth shut. I feel like I have to walk on eggshells around you! Ever since you picked up that fucking hitchhiker, our life has been a mess! Can't you see it Nick, can't you see we are being punished?'

'Don't be silly, do you seriously think other people don't go through hard times?' Nick was getting angry now.

'No, I don't think everyone does! Not like we have!' How do I even know what you told me is the truth? Maybe there is more to the story? Did you fuck him, Nick? Did you kill him on purpose? Silvia couldn't stop herself from accusing him.

'What the hell has come over you? I told you the fucking truth.' Nick grabbed both of her arms and shook her. He let her go, and stalked out of the room.

'That's right, walk out.' Silvia yelled after him.

Nick stormed back. 'I know you are grieving but don't take it out on me. I didn't kill her, and what happened in the past was an accident. Maybe I should have gone to the fucking police, but I didn't! And you didn't! I can't turn back time! I can't change anything!'

'I should have left you a long time ago.'

Nick was livid, 'Then why didn't you?'

Silvia sat sobbing, knowing in her heart she would never leave. She loved him too much.

That night, he held her in silence as they lay in bed trying to come to terms with the tragedy. Silvia was quietly holding in her feelings when tears started to spill from her eyes. His way of comforting her was to go down on her as she lay there feeling numb. Men seemed to think that sex was the cure for everything. At first she tried to resist, but soon gave way and went with the feelings of pleasure he was giving her.

Chapter 23

Life went on and Silvia returned to work. She had intended to only take a week off but decided to wait until after the funeral to go back. In herself, she felt disconnected from everyone and everything. Her coworkers thought her mood was flat which they put down to the flu. Silvia's doctor gave her a sick leave certificate which explained her absence.

All her colleagues asked how she was feeling and she answered, 'Exhausted,' which wasn't a lie. Pam bought Silvia some vitamins that she swore would get her energy back. Pam had taken them the last time she had the flu and recommended them to everyone ever since. Silvia started taking them because she felt that they couldn't hurt. She had the flu a few years back and remembered she felt like she had been hit by a bus; the way she felt now was not dissimilar.

After the first few days it was actually good to get back to work. Pam was loud and upbeat as usual and Melissa was chirpy and liked to talk about anything and everything. Jim asked Silvia to come into his office more frequently to stand there while he examined his patients. Silvia enjoyed seeing how charismatic he was in the way he interacted with them. He would look at Silvia to see her reaction, his gaze lingering a little longer than was appropriate. He was indeed flirting not only with the patients but also with Silvia. She actually enjoyed the distraction.

When she was home, her way of dealing with her grief was to put her air pods in her ears and listen to music while she performed her yoga. The music she listened to was anything but calming, people seem to think that yoga is all about calmness and stretching but Silvia used this time to connect with herself. She liked to do her yoga to Led Zeppelin, A Whole Lotta a Love and during the moaning in the song she would scream and moan out her emotions. She listened to Kaleo – Way Down We Go as she shook violently and listening to and Soko We Might Be Dead By Tomorrow, she cried. It was her way of getting everything out, to release her pent up emotions and clear her heart and mind.

Silvia began chanting and meditating every night and slowly the pain disappeared. She could no longer do her yoga poses because she had no energy or desire to do anything, but for some reason her poses gave way to chanting and meditation which was what helped her.

Winter passed and spring was in full bloom. Magic had happened. Silvia was not the same person, she was born again like a tree that loses its leaves and gives birth to new buds. A new Silvia was born, a more grounded Silvia emerged.

The tragic death of her friend changed her. It was not the only tragedy she had faced, but it happened when she was ready to embrace the learning. In that way, it was the most significant. Or was it the chanting and meditation that changed her? Whatever it was, she was experiencing less emotional attachment.

She no longer felt the need to attach herself to others; she no longer allowed things that were out of her control to affect her. She accepted the past was over and done with; the past was dead and could not be changed.

She wouldn't carry the burden any longer. Some things are never resolved or could never be resolved. She acknowledged the only way to resolve them was in your own mind and heart and that's what she did. Finally, she understood the power of the mind; to be able to control her thoughts meant she could control her emotions and her feelings. To play the past over and over again in her mind was to bring the pain or the guilt into the now which was a complete waste of existence.

She understood her mind needed to be focused on what was worthy of her focus. No longer would she allow her mind to be captured by anything unworthy. She came to the conclusion that television and social media was a ploy to capture her attention and she made a conscious decision to give her attention only to what she deemed worthy.

She knew that every moment was precious and that if she gave the moment her full attention she would be able to let it go, knowing that she lived it to the full, and there would be no regrets. Even if someone she loved died, she would know she did her best to soak them up and give them her full attention, enjoying their company while she could.

Everything was more beautiful to her now. Her garden radiated love, the people in her life, her cat, gave her pleasure in their presence and gave her life more meaning. Life was a gift that was fleeting and every moment was worthy of living to the fullest extent. She knew she could never recapture a moment and would no longer even try.

Chapter 24

Silvia was at front reception when Sally dropped into the clinic. The previous day she had sent a photo message to Silvia, it was a collage of 3 photos; the first photo was of Sally before her facelift, the second was about 2 weeks after the operation and the third was a more recent photo which was about six weeks post op. Silvia messaged her straight back, 'Wow, Sally you look amazing!'

Silvia was sincere in her message. Sally really did look great. She noticed in the first photo Sally had a slight sagging of skin below the jaw line and the skin underneath her eyes looked dark and drawn; there was sadness in her eyes. In the second photo, her face was swollen but strangely the swelling made her look younger; in this photo her eyes reflected hope. In the last photo, the swelling had come down and she looked very much the same as she did in the first photo although slightly different, Silvia couldn't quite put her finger on what the difference was, although her eyes reflected more confidence.

'Good morning Silvia, how are you?'

'I'm really good, Sally, I haven't really spoken to you since the surgery, just for a moment at Judith's birthday, how was it, was it painful?'

'No, it wasn't as bad as I thought it would be. It's the resting and the bruising that's hard, I've had lots of surgeries over the years.' She went on to tell Silvia about all of them: the two nose jobs, breast implants, a tummy tuck, coral implants in her cheeks and now a facelift, not to mention all the Botox and fillers which were a given.

Silvia couldn't believe what she was hearing. Sally went on to explain that being a plastic surgeon's wife and running the practice meant she had to relate to their clients. Of course Jim didn't do any of the surgeries on her for legal reasons; a surgeon wasn't permitted to operate on their immediate family, but at least she understood the procedures and was able to educate clients and answer any questions they might have.

Katy walked by and stopped to listen in on their conversation; she reassured Sally that she looked amazing and that all those surgeries were worth it. Katy was going overboard with her praise. She was really trying to suck up to Sally.

Since the scandal of Katy's affair, Jim had become more aloof towards her and he frequently asked Silvia to take her place in the examining room. Katy was obviously unhappy about it and her personality changed. She was more bitchy now, although not to Sally who she continued to shower with sweetness and light. But for Silvia it was the exact opposite. Katy began to micromanage her and to nitpick about small things. For instance, she listened in on Silvia's phone calls and conversations and was constantly correcting her. Silvia felt very uneasy whenever Katy was around.

Katy had stayed in her marriage and her husband forgave her for the affair. However, she held in her emotional anger towards him. He hadn't shown her the affection she needed, which was why she turned to another man. For the past few years he had been so involved with his job and playing golf that he hardly took any notice of Katy. She was jealous of the time he spent playing golf and how his commitment to his job far outweighed his commitment to her. She felt abandoned and lonely. When another man showed an interest in her, it made her feel desirable again; she was a sexy woman, not just a mother.

The affair started innocently enough, with a smile when they saw each other at the school drop off. Whenever he bumped into her at the local supermarket, they chatted effortlessly about their children and school. There was chemistry between them they couldn't deny. One day they caught up for a coffee with some of the other parents after school drop off. Perhaps it was lust or a midlife crisis or the loneliness that develops when you are treated as if you're part of the furniture. Whatever her motivation, she began an affair and it made her feel alive again. It also made her feel guilty, and somehow beautiful and ugly at the same time.

Katy had a slender athletic body more like a teenager's body than a woman's. She liked to be slim and she found running helped with stress; she would often run when her children's behaviour drove her crazy, or her husband annoyed her and since the affair she had found running to be a great way to release her guilt and anger.

She began training for different events like running for cancer or half marathons. She liked the way her body looked; being thin and athletic made her feel powerful. Knowing that their weight was an issue for so many women, she could control her weight through running; in this way she felt ever so slightly superior, not that she would ever admit it.

Katy had lost a lot of control in her life since the affair. Work had always been where she exerted full control. She knew Jim needed her expertise, and she desperately needed to be needed. She was an excellent nurse and was right beside Jim in theatre helping him with all his cases. He considered her indispensable and she was going to make sure it stayed that way.

****

Pam was in Melissa's office checking the theatre list for the next day's surgery, making sure the surgeries were in the correct order, 'That all looks hunky dory but Jim's consulting this afternoon and he may add one or two more cases,' said Pam.

'Is that Sally's voice?' Melissa asked.

'Yeah, it sounds like her; she didn't tell me she was coming in today.'

They dropped what they were doing and went into the reception area where Sally was talking with Silvia and Katy.

'You didn't tell me you were dropping in?' Pam said in a surprised voice, giving Sally a hug.

'Hi lovely, I wanted to give you each an invitation to my 50th birthday party.' As Sally finished her sentence, Claudia walked through the door, she had been to the post office to post some products to a client.

'What's going on here?' Claudia asked smiling.

Melissa chirped, 'Sally's dropped in to tell us about her 50th.'

They gathered in an excited throng around Sally who handed out their invitations.

'Thank you, Sally,' said Silvia as she received her the invitation.

'Where is it going to be held?' asked Katy.

'We decided on the Dome in Melbourne. Its architecture is so beautiful and we have about 200 guests coming. Jim wanted it to be grand affair as we are inviting a lot of surgeons and high-profile people to the party.'

'That place is beautiful, I went there years ago to a relative's wedding,' said Katy.

'Count me in,' said Claudia.

'Me too, I wouldn't miss it for the world,' Melissa added.

Melissa felt privileged to be part of Jim and Sally's life. Apart from her job at the clinic she had a very ordinary life. Her husband was a truck driver and a bit rough around the edges. When she first introduced him to Sally and Jim, she was a little embarrassed but they embraced him and her children, giving the kids Christmas gifts every year and inviting them to Christmas and birthday functions.

'Well, you know I'm coming, you old mole,' laughed Pam.

They all knew it was only Pam who could talk to Sally like that due to their long and close friendship. The others would never dare speak to her that way. Sally may have grown up in Frankston, but she certainly wasn't a Frankstonite. She was very formal in her manner and spoke with a plum in her mouth. Everyone knew that they had to suck pussy if they wanted to keep their jobs.

'Pam, I'll leave Kerri Anne's invitation with you. Could you make sure you give it to her when she comes in tomorrow?' asked Sally.

'No problem, gorgeous,' replied Pam.

Kerri Anne was often away from the office and had been away on a managerial conference in Sydney for the past three days.

A patient walked in the door so everyone glided away and went back to work while Sally went into the backroom to talk to Pam.

****

The phone rang and Katy answered it, 'Good afternoon, Jim Istible's clinic, how can I help you?'

'Hello, is Silvia there please?'

'I'm sorry, she's not here at the moment can I get her to call you back?'

'Yes please, can you tell her that Charlotte called, I'm her niece?'

'No problem,' Katy hung up the phone and scribbled a post-it note for Silvia and stuck it on Silvia's computer screen, and walked off into one of the consulting rooms.

Silvia returned from the ladies, she saw the note on her screen and called Charlotte straight back.

'Hi Charlotte, you called: is everything OK?'

'I wanted to make sure you're OK, Aunty Silv. I know you've been through a lot with Rita and all.'

'I'm fine, sweetie. Thanks for calling, I'll call you tonight.'

'That's good, I love you Aunty.'

'Love you too.'

****

Sally stayed at the clinic for the rest of the day going through some accounts with Pam. Then she had a meeting with Claudia to discuss the idea of starting a line of skin care products. They wanted to complement the whole beauty range with top-quality skin care products which they would promote alongside the Botox, fillers and micro dermabrasion.

Sally left the clinic just before the end of the day. It had been good getting back to work and seeing the girls. Her mood was light-hearted as she was looking forward to a wonderful evening with Jim, having made arrangement to go out to dinner with friends.

When Silvia got home that evening, she opened the invitation and displayed it on the fridge door.

Fifty & Fabulous
Cocktail Party
Silvia & Nick
You are invited to attend the celebration of
Sally Istible's 50th birthday
19 November @ 6p.m.
The Dome
333 Collins Street
Melbourne

Nick looked at the invitation, 'Mmm, looks like it'll be an interesting night.'

'Yeah, it should be fun. I'm looking forward to it. You will meet my work colleagues. Jim's a bit of a flirt, his wife Sally is lovely.'

'A bit of a flirt hey,' Nick said with a cheeky grin.

'Yes Nick, are you jealous?' replied Silvia laughing.

'No, not at all, have I reason to be?'

'Oh shut up.' Silvia laughed.

I'm looking forward to flirting with his wife.'

'Sure you are.' Silvia disregarded his cheekiness, 'I think I like Judith the most, she's one of the nurses. Pam and Melissa are friendly too, but lately Katy has acted like a real bitch.'

'What has she been doing or saying?'

'She's started listening in on my conversations and corrects me while I'm talking to patients. She never used to be like that but it's as if she's trying to make me look stupid to big note herself or something.'

'Don't let her get to you, you know your job.'

'Yeah I know. Hey, we should book a hotel room in the city on that night. Then we can have a few drinks without having to drive home, what do you think?'

'Sounds good to me, I'm always up for a night in the city.'

'Terrific! I'll look online to see what hotels are within walking distance of The Dome.'

Chapter 25

Jim sat waiting for Sally to come downstairs. They had dinner arrangements and she always took a long time getting ready. He poured himself a Scotch as his mind wandered into the past; he recalled sitting on his mother's bed watching her as she brushed her hair, he must have been around six years old.

She was sitting at her dressing table with her back to him. He watched her as she brushed her long dark hair which fell like waves of silk around her shoulders and neck.

'Do you think I'm beautiful, Jamie?' she asked as she looked into the mirror. 'Do you think mummy is pretty?'

She was beautiful with her creamy skin, dark blue eyes and rosy cheeks. He could see her reflection in the mirror and couldn't understand why she was asking him such a question.

Jamie had pains in his stomach; he kept going to the lavatory, and was feeling weak and nauseous. He wanted his mother to hug him and tell him everything would be alright but couldn't articulate his feelings.

He held in his pain and declared, 'Of course you are, mummy, you are the most beautiful lady in the world.'

Once he told her what she wanted to hear, he hoped she would pay attention to him, and see that he was in pain. She just continued brushing her hair with sadness in her eyes.

'You're just saying that, you don't really mean it,' she said, lost in her own thoughts.

Jamie tried to jump off the bed and run to the bathroom, but he was too late and vomited all over the bedspread and some of the vomit splashed onto the carpet. As he ran, he felt as though he had peed but it was actually diarrhea.

'Oh God help me!' his mother yelled. 'Why didn't you tell me you were going to be sick you stupid—' she stopped short of calling him an idiot.

His mother told him to strip off his clothes and she dragged him into the shower. Turning on the cold tap she threw his soiled clothes in. Jamie was crying and cowering in the corner of the shower which was freezing. Finally, she turned on the hot tap and, when the water was warm enough, he crawled under it. The warmth of the water calmed him and he felt more comforted by the water than by his own mother.

'Wash those dirty clothes while I go and clean up the bedspread. What's your father going to say when he sees this stain on the carpet?' she muttered angrily.

Jamie soaked in the comfort of the warm water running down his back. Crying, he picked up the soap, which kept slipping out of his grip, as he tried to clean his underwear. While he was showering, he pondered his mother's words, - "What's your father going to say when he sees this stain on the carpet?" His father wouldn't care about the stain on the carpet. If anything, his father would hug him and tell him everything was going to be OK.

He loved his father more than anything. He was a kind, quiet man. As he was an investigative journalist, he travelled for weeks at a time, but when he was home he was a loving father. He would sit with Jamie at night and tell him all kinds of stories about the places he had been and the famous people he had interviewed.

Jamie loved his mother too, but he could never please her, nothing he did for her was ever enough. No amount of telling her how beautiful she was could ever convince her of her beauty. She was a needy woman who had no self-confidence. She believed all she had going for her were her looks, but her looks had started to fade. She had no self-belief on which to draw. Her self-talk was always negative and abusive, she felt powerless and her inner dialogue was one of hatred towards herself. She hated her body, she felt ugly and she felt guilty for being inadequate as a mother. She felt guilty if she said the wrong thing to someone. She would replay conversations over and over in her mind. She would find fault in others and liked to gossip. If she heard a bad story on the news, she would call her friends to fill them in on the bad news.

She didn't know how to change the record in her mind to a new and brighter one. She loved her husband and she loved Jamie but she was jealous of the freedom her husband had, and she felt resentment that she had to stay at home and look after Jamie while her husband travelled the world. Deep down, she didn't trust her husband and suspected him of having an affair, because she couldn't understand why he would want to be with someone like her.

Jim grew up feeling the need to make women feel good about themselves. He knew the importance of beauty and that's why he became one of the best cosmetic surgeons in the business. He had the power to make people feel good about themselves, or at least he thought he did.

Sally walked in and Jim's mind snapped back to the present. She was wearing tight leather pants and a leopard print shirt, her lips painted burnt orange, her eyes dark and beautiful. Not to spoil her makeup, he went to kiss her neck and his hand reached down to her crotch. Sally cringed at the thought of sex; she was annoyed that he couldn't even kiss her without him wanting sex.

'Not now Jim, we're about to go out.'

'I know but we haven't done it for weeks and you look so sexy.' In Jim's mind, he thought he was flattering her.

'I haven't been feeling well, you know that, and we're just about to go out. Bloody hell, do you want me to take another hour to get ready, we'll be late?'

'Of course not, darling, let's get going,' Jim kissed her forehead and gave her a slap on the bum as she turned to pick up her hand bag.

Sally gave him a cheeky smile, 'When we get home, if you're lucky, I'll give you a blow job.'

'I'm feeling lucky,' he replied with his toothy smile.

The promise of a blow job was highly unlikely to be fulfilled, because after a night out she'd say she's too tired or she would be too drunk. Jim tried to get through to her not to drink so much. He didn't understand why she couldn't be happy with a couple of drinks and pace herself. She didn't get drunk all the time, just when she was with close friends, but it annoyed him because he expected her to be more classy than being the party drunk.

Jim felt guilty wanting sex from Sally lately. He began to withdraw from even trying, he would just wank himself more often than not. He had begun to feel unloved. He enjoyed his rendezvous in Byron Bay with Bob but that was just lust. He really loved Sally and needed to feel close to her. He longed for some flirtation and passion again, but they seemed to be drifting apart.

Jim met Bob at a plastic surgeons' convention in Sydney and they hit it off straight away. Bob was a sales rep for a pharmaceutical company. He asked Jim to have a drink with him after the convention to talk more business. One thing led to another and they ended up in bed. Jim had always fantasised about having sex with another man and when Bob made a pass at him he was flattered. He felt alive like never before, the excitement of having a secret life made him feel free, sexy and alive.

Bob was about 10 years younger than he was which excited Jim. He was no longer young and to have Bob want him made him feel powerful again. For Bob, it was Jim's prestige and money that was exciting, and to be Jim's lover made him feel closer to getting the things he wanted in life.

When Jim found himself in bed with Bob the first time, the lust and the sex was exhilarating. He felt exuberant for days, even weeks afterward, and so they began having monthly rendezvous. When Bob came to Melbourne for business, he would drop by the clinic to see Jim. If Bob dropped in, Jim would tell Pam to reschedule the next couple of appointments. Having sex with Bob in his office brought the excitement to a new level, even though the exhilaration Jim initially felt had worn off.

Chapter 26

Silvia woke up with a start. Her phone was ringing. Who would be calling at 2.30a.m.on a Friday morning? She reached out for it, a tightness in her chest. She saw it was Ted and took the call, 'Is everything alright?'

'Silvia, Phoebe's waters have broken,' Ted's voice bellowed on the other end of the phone 'she's having strong contractions.'

'Oh my God how exciting! How strong, have you been timing them?'

'I'm not sure but they're getting stronger, sometimes 20 minutes apart, then 12 minutes, and now 10.'

Silvia could hear Phoebe groaning in the background.

'What are you waiting for? Take her to the hospital! We'll meet you there. It won't take us long to get ready.'

'OK, OK,' he kept repeating, his breathing loud and ragged. Obviously Ted was trying to calm himself down.

'Ted, keep calm, and drive Phoebe to the hospital.' Silvia took charge of the situation, reminding him. 'And drive carefully; she's depending on you to get her there safely.' She couldn't bear if they were in an accident on the way to the hospital. It would be a nightmare and she had more than enough nightmares already. Silvia reached out her arm to nudge Nick's shoulder, making sure he was awake.

Nick was sitting up in bed, rubbing his eyes, listening to Silvia. She hung up the phone and jumped out of bed.

'Quick, get dressed, Phoebe's having the baby.'
Silvia threw on a pair of jeans and an old, but comfy, dark blue knitted jumper that was lying on the chair next to her bed. She tied her hair into a bun on top of her head and gave her face a quick wash, patting her cheeks to wake herself up.

Nick was already dressed but couldn't find his keys, yelling out to Silvia, 'Do you know where my keys are, honey?' and 'Where did I put those bloody keys?' He lifted a few papers off the kitchen bench, no not there. Walking into the living room, he pulled back the cushions on the sofa, and slid his hand behind them. Had they slipped out of his pocket when he was watching TV?

'No, I've told you to keep them in one spot, you're always losing your keys,' she yelled back at him, applying some lip gloss and shading in her eyebrows. Being blond she felt bald without her eyebrows shaded in. She had toyed with the idea of having them tattooed on but couldn't bring herself to trust anyone to do a good job.

'I found them!'

'Thank God,' Silvia let out a loud sigh, 'Where were they?'

'They had fallen off the dining table. I must remember to put them on the key hook next time,' Nick reminded himself.

'Can you make us a quick coffee Nick; I need to wake up properly?'

'Sure, honey.' Now he had found his keys he could relax a little.

Silvia could hear Nick turning on the coffee machine; she walked into the kitchen and gave Nick a hug from behind as he was preparing the coffee. In that moment she felt a great thankfulness wash over her. Nick was always there for her. He turned around and they stood there with their arms around each other.

'I'm so excited for Phoebe, and so happy she wants me to be with her in the delivery room.' Phoebe would have wanted her mother to be with her but she was so close to Silvia, who was like a mother to her.

'Why wouldn't she want you there, you're a beautiful person and will be a great comfort for her.'

Silvia looked up at Nick and kissed him.

'Come on, honey, let's get going, we can drink the coffee on the way to the hospital,' said Nick.

In the car they sat in silence, Silvia looked out of her window as Nick drove. She was full of excitement, tinged with some anxiety. She had never had the opportunity to witness a baby being born. She had once seen a birth on a documentary and thought it was so beautiful, but had never seen one in real life.

The roads were empty; daylight was a few hours away. She watched as they drove past houses with the street lights on. In the background she could hear the hum of distant trucks driving along the freeway. Most people would be tucked up in their warm beds. That time of morning felt calm and serene to Silvia and she wondered if it was why most babies are born in the early hours of the morning.

She imagined how she would have felt if she was on her way to hospital to have her own baby. A mantle of sadness crept over her. She had longed to have a child but after years of trying, eventually she gave up her dream of being a mother, and now here she was going to witness her niece Phoebe give birth. She was blessed; at least she could be at the birth of this child. Her thoughts flipped in an instant. One word clanged inside her head, 'Sean' who never had the chance to be a father or an uncle.

She turned to Nick, 'Nick, I know you don't want to talk about what happened, all those years ago, you know to Sean but….'

Nick cringed, 'Silvia, why now? Why would you bring it up? Nothing can change what happened. This is a happy time. Please, honey, don't upset yourself by dragging up the past.'

'You're right, I'm sorry,' she turned and looked out of the window. A large sign indicated the hospital car park was ahead. Hospital Staff Left, Public Parking Straight Ahead.

Nick took Silvia's hand and brought it to his lips, kissing her hand gently. He drove into the hospital car park. After locating a convenient bay, he stopped the car and turned to Silvia.

'You think I haven't agonized over what happened to Sean and the pain I've caused you. I've been dying inside ever since it happened. But I can't change it, Silvia.' Nick's voice was weak and trembling. He hunched over the steering wheel, his head bent low as if he was praying.

'I know, Nick, I know.' Silvia felt waves of emotion welling up inside. 'I'm truly sorry for bringing it up, I had no intention of—' she paused and continued, 'I hadn't thought about him for ages and when I think I'm OK, that I've let it go, something will trigger me and I'm back in that dark place again.'

'I don't know what you want me to say,' Nick lifted his head up and looked into Silvia's eyes. She met his gaze: he was the man she loved and that had not changed, but now she couldn't help but see the weakness in him. She pitied him and wanted to protect him from being brought to account for what happened that night

Silvia reached across, placing her hands on either side of his face, and kissed him with great tenderness. She whispered, 'Let's go in, my love, we have a baby to meet.'

****

Ted was waiting for them outside the delivery room. They could see his excitement from a mile away. He reached for Nick's hand and shook it vigorously.

Silvia gave him a quick kiss, 'Is shc OK, can I go in?'
'Yes go in.'

In the delivery room, Phoebe, was looking a little scared but her expression transformed as soon as she saw Silvia. Her relief was instant. Tears welled up in both their eyes as they gave each other an extra-long hug.

'You'll be OK, Phoebe, think of how many people there are in this world,' Silvia gently reassured her, 'It couldn't be too hard.'

Forty five minutes later, Charlotte arrived and the two of them comforted and encouraged Phoebe through the contractions. They took it in turns to rub her lower back. Charlotte even looked up a You Tube video on easing the pain through pressure points in the hand and back. It seemed to work, but then a new wave of pain came on.

Nurses came in regularly to check how many centimetres her cervix had dilated. Minutes before she was about to start pushing, the doctor arrived; he was wearing white gum boots and a white apron.

Silvia was amazed by his appearance, "Bloody hell, he looks more like a butcher than a doctor," but she kept her opinion to herself.

Charlotte and Silvia were on either side of Phoebe holding her hands as she pushed this beautiful miracle out. Overcome with joy, they cried, laughed and cooed at Phoebe's baby boy who bellowed his hello to the world. It was a wonderful moment for all of them.

Nathanial she named him, Nathanial Marcus. The name just popped right out of her mouth for no apparent reason, but it suited him to a tee. She had gone into labour a week early but he really didn't need to be in there any longer. He was a big boy with a head of hair.

Silvia and Charlotte sat with Phoebe for about an hour, mesmerised by the little boy. A nurse came in and asked Phoebe if she would like to have a shower. Charlotte helped Phoebe shower and put on some fresh clothes while Silvia held Nathanial. He was so beautifully delicious, she kissed him all over his face and rubbed her cheek against his cheek, feeling his soft skin against her skin.

As she stared at him, he yawned and opened his eyes, and Silvia found herself overcome with love and gratitude. This little boy was a part of her and she resolved to love and protect him as if he was her own baby.

Ted and Nick waited until Phoebe was given a room in the ward.

To their delight, they took it in turns to hold Nathanial. Ted held him first and then handed him to Nick. Silvia had to laugh because they both held him in that awkward way men hold newborns, as though they were scared they would break him.

Chapter 27

Once Phoebe settled back at home with Nathanial, Ted arranged a Sunday lunch to welcome his grandson into the world. Jarrod had returned home from his trip so it was the perfect excuse for a family gathering.

It turned out to be a beautiful spring day. Ted and Silvia's parents were the first to arrive; they were doting over Nathanial. Having mellowed in their old age, they loved to be at family gatherings, always being the first to arrive and the last to leave.

Charlotte and her boyfriend arrived with a selection of cakes which she had arranged beautifully on a decorative cake tray. She made room for them on the kitchen table then gave her father Ted and Helena a kiss hello. Her boyfriend had already shaken hands with Ted and couldn't get outside quick enough to see Jarrod who was barbequing skewers of prawns and chicken.

Phoebe had opened a bottle of champagne and poured a glass for Charlotte and Helena. 'What about you, Mormor, would you like a glass?' she asked her grandmother.

'Oh yes of course I would, this is a celebration.' Her grandmother acted as though she loved a glass of champagne, but she really didn't like the taste of alcohol. She pretended to like it, just to look the part. She would sip at it, and when no one was looking she would tip it into a pot plant or down the sink.

'What about you, Morfar?' asked Phoebe.

'Not for me, thanks, I'll have a beer with the boys later,' replied her grandfather.

Phoebe poured a glass for her grandmother and placed it on a small table beside her chair. Her grandmother had been holding Nathanial for the past half hour and her grandfather had been pulling funny faces trying to get him to smile. 'I can't believe he's already 4 weeks old. He's a big boy; he has his great grandfather's good looks,' joked Phoebe's grandfather puffing out his chest.

Phoebe laughed, enjoying her grandfather's sense of humour. There was a knock at the door, Phoebe excused herself and went to see who it was, Nick and Silvia had arrived.

'Hi Phoebe, how are you feeling?' Nick asked as he kissed her on her cheek and stood back to admire her. She looked like a proud new mother.

'If you really want to know, my boobs have been driving me nuts,' she laughed. 'I'm not used to having enormous boobs that leak and cracked nipples. Otherwise, I'm great, he's been so good and he's sleeping well, he's just gorgeous.'

'Well, you look fantastic, Phoebe,' said Nick.

Silvia's hands were full of gifts for Phoebe and Nathanial. 'These are for you and bub,' she had bought Nathanial a cute little outfit from Boss Kids, it was way too expensive but she couldn't help herself. For Phoebe, she bought a gift voucher for a spa treatment and massage. She thought the new mum might need the pampering after everything she had been through; giving birth was not for the faint hearted.

Phoebe accepted the gifts and hugged Silvia, 'Thank you, Aunty; Mormor and Morfar are here already, they are with Nathanial. Mormor doesn't want to let him go,' laughed Phoebe as she pointed to her grandmother who was sitting in the comfy reclining chair holding Nathanial.

Silvia rushed over to see Nathanial, 'Isn't he a darling?' she cooed as she gave her father a kiss hello, and put her arm around her mother. 'You'll scare him with all those silly faces you're pulling, Dad.'

'He's a little angel,' replied her mother.

'Don't be silly, didn't you see him smiling at me,' replied her father.

Helena asked if they would like to go outside. She had arranged the garden table beautifully and wanted to show it off. It was set up with flowers, candles and platters of fruit and cheese.

Nick's parents were also invited. They arrived with a selection of Greek goodies, including stuffed vine leaves and a tray of moussaka, along with gifts for the baby.

Ted was helping Helena in the kitchen sorting out the salads and meat, the two of them brought everything out to the table. Jarrod was in charge of cooking and Charlotte's boyfriend was supervising. Once the meat was cooked, everyone sat down to eat. Nick filled their glasses with red wine and Ted gave a toast, 'To happy days everyone, I love you all and cheers to Nathanial Marcus.'

Everyone cheered and clicked their glasses, thinking that was all Ted was going to say.

'And,' Ted cleared his throat with a little cough, 'I'm grateful the whole family could be here today, and that Jarrod is safely home from his trip after all these months.'

'Good to see you, mate,' said Nick placing his hand on Jarrod's shoulder and squeezing it.

It was a beautiful spring day and the atmosphere was one of happiness and joy.

After lunch, Jarrod took out his guitar and began strumming and singing a song called Home by Sam Garrett. Jarrod looked happy and healthy; all that travelling had obviously been beneficial. His skin was tanned, his hair was long and tied up in a man bun. He had adopted the unshaven look which made him look pretty cool. His Swedish genes with those light blue-grey eyes gave him a presence that commanded attention.

It was a good day, one of those days that made life worth living.

Chapter 28

Melissa arrived at work, whirling through the door with a box of assorted Krispy Kreme donuts. She placed one on a tissue beside Silvia as she usually did on a Monday morning.

'Thank you, Melissa,' said Silvia.

Every time Melissa brought in the donuts, Silvia would do the same thing, thank her politely and break it in half and either throw the other half in the bin when no one was looking, or wrap the other half in the tissue and take it home for Nick. Sometimes she would only have a quarter depending on how she was feeling. It was kind of Melissa to bring them in, although Silvia didn't like eating too many sweets. Not wanting to hurt Melissa's feelings or to make her uncomfortable, she would accept it graciously.

Everyone liked Melissa but she didn't like herself enough, and often put herself down. If she caught an image of herself walking past a shop window, she would say, oh God I'm looking fat, or, look at my double chin, or, God I'm getting old and ugly. To compensate she would walk around the shopping centre to buy something to make her feel better. She would walk through Target or Myer and pick up a handful of clothes and try them on, but would feel even worse because she didn't look good in the clothes.

She would look at jewellery or perfume instead, because jewellery and perfume didn't make you look awful. She needed that fix, something to buy, something to take home to fill her emptiness. If she didn't buy something, she would feel like a failure. At other times, she would go to the hairdresser's and ask them to choose a style for her, because she didn't know what she wanted or what suited her.

That particular day everyone started talking about Sally's forthcoming birthday party.

'What are you going to wear, Pam?' asked Melissa.

'I've just bought the most gorgeous gown, it's green with a shawl to match, but I still have to find some shoes to go with it. What about you, lovely, what are you going to wear, have you found anything yet?'

'I was thinking of the dress I wore to my niece's wedding last year. When I tried it on last night, it's a bit tight. I think I'm not going to eat carbs for a few weeks or maybe try one of those shake diets.'

'Apparently, Aldi has good shakes, and they aren't very expensive.' Pam said.

'They don't work,' Silvia chimed in. 'You have to change your eating habits. The other day I was listening to a talk by J.Krishnamurti on how to break free of habits. Maybe you should listen to it: it's on YouTube; it's about being present and observing yourself in the moment. It is how to distance yourself from what your mind believes to be reality. You have to take a step back and look at yourself without judgment and observe yourself and what you do without attachment.'

Pam thought Silvia was a bit whacky with some of the things she came out with. It must be all that yoga stuff she's into and arty people often were a bit weird. She would tell Melissa not to take too much notice of what Silvia said, but she would say it in private. She didn't want to offend Silvia, not to her face anyway.

'Yeah, those diets don't work, you'll just put it all back on again, plus more. Claudia said.

Why don't you just buy a new dress and love the person you are now, instead of trying to be who you were last year,' said Silvia.

'Mmm you're right; I should just go and buy a new dress.'

'Maybe we can go shopping this Saturday? I still haven't decided what to wear,' said Claudia.

'Sounds like a plan, what about you Silvia? Do you have a dress to wear; do you want to come with us?'

'Yes, I have two dresses in mind, depending on the weather. One's red with long sleeves and the other's a pink short-sleeved dress. I would have loved to come with you, it sounds like it will be a fun day out, but I've made plans to meet with my art supplier on Saturday.'

Silvia really didn't want to go, for some reason she didn't feel like she fit in with them. She liked her own small group of family and friends and didn't want to get too close to the people she worked with, not in a social setting anyway.

'We can always go the following Saturday,' replied Claudia.

'No, don't be silly, you two go and enjoy yourselves.'

The phone rang.

'Good morning, Jim Istible's clinic how can I help you, this is Silvia speaking?'

'Hello Silvia, is Sally there?'

'No, Sally isn't in the office. She'll be in soon, can I give her a message'.

'I tried calling her mobile but she didn't answer. Can you let her know her brother John called, and that Pat needs some Botox to manage the migraines, she will know what I mean.'

'No problem, John, I'll pass on the message.'

'Thanks Silvia,' John said.

When she breezed into reception, Sally arrived holding a basket filled with gifts for everyone, she handed Silvia a box wrapped in beautiful green Damask wrapping paper with a little card that read:

'Thank-you for being part of our team
& the great work you've done'
♥ *Sally & Jim*

She proceeded to give one to everyone. Pam's was in red gift wrapping, Melissa's in yellow, Claudia's in pink and Kerri Anne's in crimson. Judith wasn't at work that day but she had one for Judith as well in orange.

'Thank you Sally, can we open it now?' asked Melissa.

'Of course you can,' Sally answered.

Silvia opened her gift first; it was a bottle of Christian Dior Jadore perfume. Then the others opened their gifts, they were all given a bottle of one of the Christian Dior perfumes.

Silvia was astonished, 'I didn't realise that Christian Dior made so many perfumes.'

'Yeah, same here,' said Melissa.

In the midst of the excitement, Silvia remembered John's message.

'Sally, I almost forgot, your brother John called saying Pat needs some Botox. He said you would know what he was talking about.'

'When did he call?'

'About half an hour before you came in,' replied Silvia.

'Oh OK, Pat must be having migraines again. I'll tell Jim to drop by their house after work tonight, thanks Silvia.'

Sally didn't stay long, she had just dropped in to give everyone their gift and to talk to Pam and Claudia about the new skin care range.

After Sally left, Melissa started a conversation with Silvia, pointing out how lucky they were to work for Sally and Jim. They always gave the staff beautiful gifts, especially around Christmas time. Last Christmas she was given a Pandora bracelet with a beautiful birthstone bead to go on it, plus a bottle of French champagne. Not only that, they were all taken out for dinner to an Italian restaurant at the Crown Casino. Silvia was impressed; in her previous job she was lucky if she received a box of chocolates.

Throughout the day, they continued talking about diets and food and Sally's up-coming 50th birthday party.

The phone rang, 'Good afternoon, Jim Istible's clinic how can I help you, this is Silvia speaking?'

'Oh, hi Silvia, it's Sally I forgot to tell Jim that John called. His mobile is off because he's consulting. Can you pass the message onto him for me?'

'Of course Sally, no problem,' replied Silvia.

Jim was consulting that afternoon; it was a busy day at the clinic. Silvia was called into his office quite a few times; she stood there while Jim examined the patient's boobs or abdomen or another part of their body. It was standard practice to have another female in the room to make sure there would be no accusations of misconduct. Silvia was feeling more and more uncomfortable with his flirtations. Was she reading too much into it? Was Jim really flirting with her or was it just his personality?

Jim had finished consulting and was about to leave when Silvia stopped him.

'Jim, Sally asked me to pass you on a message. John called earlier today and asked if you could stop by and give Pat some Botox to help with the migraines.'

'Oh, Pat's migraines are getting worse,' Jim mumbled to himself. 'Thanks Silv, you have a good night and don't do anything I wouldn't do.' he said with a mischievous smile. He went to the back room and took out a vial of Botox from the fridge and left.

Silvia pondered his words as she switched on the ignition of her car. It had been an interesting day at work, there was always something happening, and no two days were the same. It was fun working at the clinic, and maybe she should lighten up about Jim's flirtations and treat them as a bit of fun too.

****

It was time to close the clinic, everyone had left except Melissa. She often stayed back to catch up with any last minute changes to the theatre list and she would lock up.

Checking that no one was around, Melissa opened Claudia's door. She took the key from the drawer where Claudia hid it under some envelopes, and opened the glass cabinet containing the various facial creams. Her heart was beating fast. She heard a noise. Did someone walk in through the reception door? She went through into the waiting room but no one was there. She checked the reception and the other rooms. Was she just hearing things? She looked out the window and into the car park. One of the doctors from the rooms next door was leaving and saying goodbye to his receptionist who was getting into her car.

Relieved, Melissa locked the door and closed the blinds. She tidied up the waiting room, putting the magazines back into the rack and emptied the waste bin. She went back into Claudia's room, searching through the cabinet, she found what she was looking for, some samples of face cream that Claudia gave to her clients. No one will notice if I take a few, she told herself. She was about to close the cabinet when she couldn't help herself, she snatched up an Aspect Starter Kit which was an antioxidant enriched collection of cleanser and exfoliate worth about $140.

She quickly locked the cabinet door and placed the key back into the drawer. She scanned the room, making sure everything was in its proper place, before walking out and closing the door behind her.

Melissa justified her actions by telling herself it wasn't really stealing. She was the one who worked the extra hours. She deserved to be compensated for all that she did. She had been doing it once in a while, at first it was only the samples but recently she was taking products that were to be sold to customers. She wouldn't get caught, she reassured herself, as she put her prize into the bottom of her bag and threw her lunch box and drink bottle on top.

Chapter 29

'What's going on Pat, your migraines seem to be getting worse? Is something triggering them?' Jim asked as he filled the syringe with Botox.

'Sorry Jim, I don't really want to talk about it.' Pat was sitting in a darkened room with the blinds drawn. Even though Pat had been having migraines for years now, they were becoming more frequent of late. Thank God for Jim suggesting the Botox injections which had really helped.

'I understand if you don't want to talk to me about it, but you do need to speak to someone,' Jim shrugged his shoulders. 'I've heard of patients getting good results from acupuncture. It can help with muscle relaxation and it could even help with gaining more clarity. I've also heard that a change of diet can make a difference, perhaps you could see a dietician, it's worth looking into.'

Pat looked up and gave a gentle nod, 'Thank you Jim, maybe I should try acupuncture.'

'For now I'll write you a script for Panadine Forte,' Jim put the empty vial into his bag and wrote out the script. 'You get some rest,' he gave Pat a hug and left the room, going to find John.

He found him in the kitchen. 'Thanks for coming around, Jim, I really appreciate your help.'

'Not at all John, I'm only too happy to help.' Sally's family looked up to Jim; when Sally started dating him, they couldn't believe it. Her family were more into trade school than university degrees, so for Sally to be dating someone above her league was quite impressive. They thought she had hit the jackpot. Jim enjoyed the boost to his ego and the feeling of superiority although he had to admit he knew nothing about plumbing or carpentry.

John's expertise had helped Jim out on numerous occasions. One infamous incident was when Jim's daughter Charlotte turned fifteen, she had a slumber party with five girlfriends staying the night and they clogged the toilet with tampons and too much toilet paper. It was Uncle John who came to the rescue.

'Pat's been getting more agitated of late, especially since some memories are coming back. Do you want a beer or a Scotch?'

'Not for me,' Jim waved his hand. 'I've had a big day at the clinic. I just want to get home, have a good meal, and then maybe I'll have a drink.'

'Come on Jim, just one.'

Jim relented, 'OK, I'll have a Scotch on the rocks,' Jim could sense John wanted the company, 'just one.'

John opened the fridge and took out a tray of ice blocks, leaving them on the bench while he went into the other room to collect two crystal glasses and a bottle of Johnny Walker from his bar. He returned to the kitchen and carefully squeezed 3 ice cubes out of the plastic ice tray and into each glass. He poured two shots of whiskey over the ice. He handed Jim the drink, glad to have his company. Pat had been acting a little strange of late and John wanted to talk to someone.

'You know how much I love Pat but lately things haven't been the same. It's as though something has triggered a memory of something in the past. Pat is withdrawn and doesn't want to confide in me. I really don't know what to think anymore.' John shook his head as if to clear his troubled thoughts and looked over to Jim as if he expected some wise advice.

'I don't know what to say, John, it's not my field, but I do know that trauma from a childhood experience or a traumatic event can cause physical or mental illness, or in Pat's case the migraines. Perhaps Pat needs to talk to someone, maybe see a psychiatrist?' Jim sipped his Scotch.

'I don't know about a psychiatrist, for migraines?'

'I don't have an answer for you John, but as I said to Pat, perhaps acupuncture could help or a change in diet. In my opinion talking to a psychiatrist may bring out more of Pat's past, but as to whether it would be better to let things lie, I simply don't know.' Jim swallowed the last of his Scotch.

'Do you want another one?'

'No, no, I have to go.' Jim's tone was firm, having only accepted the drink because John had insisted.

'I'll have a talk to Pat, thanks again Jim,' John shook Jim's hand.

'I'm sure Pat will be OK, don't worry too much,' Jim walked towards the door to leave, and remembered. He swung about, 'Oh and by the way, it's not long until Sally's 50th there will be a lot of interesting characters attending. I'm sure you two will enjoy it. I know you both like to mingle, and have a good reason to get dressed up, especially Pat,' Jim winked and turned to open the door.

'Thanks Jim, yeah we're looking forward to it.'

****

Some months prior, Pat had been at the clinic for a series of Botox injections and was about to leave when an attractive woman with burgundy shoulder-length hair caught Pat's eye. She was sitting in a car right outside Jim Istible's clinic. Her head was down and she appeared to be reading. At that moment, the sign on the side of the car door – NicksCS - triggered a memory.

Pat sat in the car for about ten minutes and studied the woman. What was she doing, she must be waiting for someone. Moments later, a petite blond woman came out of the clinic. She was wearing a black dress with a lacy pink scarf and was clutching a leopard print cardigan. She wasted no time, walking briskly to the waiting car and getting into the passenger seat.

The two women sat talking for a while before driving out of the car park. In that instant Pat decided to follow them. They pulled into a car park near a lake and went into a restaurant, the sign above the entrance said Rosie's.

Pat remained in the car, almost as if in a trance and studied the car and its signage, NicksCS. The voluptuous woman with burgundy hair came out of the restaurant talking loudly on her phone, waving her hands in the air. She was animated, perhaps even distressed. After a moment or two, she put her phone into her bag. A man came over and gave her a hug and a quick kiss. The woman went back into the restaurant and the man walked right past Pat to reach his car, which also had the sign NicksCS, on the side of the door.

Pat's heartbeat increased. Years had passed but the man looked familiar?

Pat waited trying to put together the memories that were flashing, disjointed but vivid. The women came out of the restaurant but Pat didn't notice they had switched seats and now the blond one was driving.

Pat followed the car to a more rural area; it turned up a long driveway towards an old wooden house.

Pat drove past the entrance and made a U turn, parking the car down the road and sat waiting, assuming it must be where Nick lived.

The mobile phone rang. The incoming call was from Pat's husband John.

'Hello John, I'm sorry I forgot to tell you I had to get a few things from the grocery store, I'll be home soon.'

'I was worried about you, are you OK? I thought you were going to the clinic and coming straight home.'

'Sorry, I was a little distracted, I won't be long.'

'Don't be sorry, take your time, I just wanted to see if you were all right, love you.'

'I love you too.'

Pat started the car and drove off, only to return on a cold winter's day.

Chapter 30

Silvia made arrangements to meet up with her art supplier in Prahran on Saturday. She wanted to buy a new easel. Her tabletop easel was suitable for smaller paintings but she wanted an A-frame easel that tilts vertically for larger canvases, and she needed new paints and brushes.

Silvia did most of her painting at home now; Betty had cut her classes down over the years and only ran classes in the summer months. During winter she travelled either up north or overseas chasing the warmer weather. Silvia didn't really need to learn much more about techniques, but she continued to attend Betty's classes because she enjoyed her company as well as the other people in the class. A warm camaraderie had developed in the group of likeminded amateur artists. Although they didn't catch up outside of class, each year they returned with interesting stories about what they had been doing during the year.

One woman had been to Africa on a safari and a cruise, and came back telling them all about the exotic animals she had seen. She went on to say the cruise was a little sad because four people died.

When Silvia first started painting, she used water colours and acrylics but had recently moved to oil painting which was challenging at first but quickly became her preferred medium. She loved experimenting with all the techniques she had learnt over the years. She took a playful approach and was not afraid to try out new things with colour and texture such as scumbling which creates more depth in a painting, or wet on wet where the paint was applied without letting earlier layers dry.

She also liked the chiaroscuro technique which originated from the Renaissance period where artists would create strong contrasts between light and dark to give a three dimensional effect.

Because of Silvia's playfulness with her paintings, she had become very confident with her technique which was essential when painting in oils. Before she set out to paint her portrait, she studied various techniques and decided she liked the use of charcoal to map out the lines of her head and face. She used a fixative so the lines wouldn't rub out. Then she built up the colours starting from dark to light.

She liked to use palette knives for a lot of her work but she also liked good quality brushes and a new range of brushes was being stocked by her art supplier. Silvia was excited to see what other new products were available.

Silvia called Charlotte to let her know that she would pop in after seeing her supplier. Charlotte's townhouse wasn't far from Prahran and it was a good excuse to see her.

She left early in the morning and arrived just as the shop opened. George, the owner greeted her like a friend, taking her by the arm to show her the easel. It was a small warehouse but it was packed from floor to ceiling with products.

'Darling, I have to show you the easel I put away for you,' George said excitedly. He acted as though he was proud of himself.

'Have a look, it's a Mont Marte made of beechwood. It would be perfect for you, darling. What do you think?'

Silvia studied it, 'I love how it has the ability to tilt completely flat, and that it has castor wheels so I can move it around to catch the perfect angle of light.'

'My thoughts exactly, and what do you think about the colour of the wood, isn't it divine?' George was a larger than life character; he wasn't an artist but he loved arty things. The easel he was showing Silvia was not one he would want for himself, he had his own collection. His pride and joy being an antique Victorian Eastlake rosewood easel that he bought at an auction. He had acquired it purely for its beauty.

'I do like it; you always seem to know exactly what I'm looking for.'

'That's my job, darling,' George smiled taking her by the arm and directing her to the new range of brushes.

Silvia met George through Betty. George was hosting an art exhibition for a friend of his, and he invited Betty and her students to come along, it was held at George's house. His partner, Henrico, wasn't as flamboyant as George, in his personality but he did dress to impress.

He made them all feel very welcome. They were greeted with champagne and air kisses at the door and given a tour of the house. It was decorated with the most interesting artifacts, and once they were directed into the studio, they couldn't help but admire the collection of antique easels standing with exquisite paintings on display.

'I've everything I need for now,' Silvia paid for her items and George carefully wrapped the easel and brushes in cloth. 'Say hi to Henrico for me, won't you?'

'Of course I will, darling.'

George helped Silvia load the easel and brushes into her car boot, 'Au revoir my, darling.'

'Thanks George, Au revoir until next time.'

****

She beeped her horn when she arrived at Charlotte's and a minute later, the garage door went up and Silvia drove in. Charlotte came running downstairs to greet her aunty.
'Hi Aunty,' Charlotte had been looking forward to catching up.

'Hello beautiful,' Silvia responded.

'Come upstairs I'll put the kettle on, or would you rather go out to a café?'

'I'll come up for a bit,' replied Silvia, 'and why don't we pop out later, to the café with the luscious cakes, my shout.'

Charlotte filled the kettle with filtered water and switched it on. She showed Silvia her latest acquisition: a set of tea cups she had just bought from T2. They were a beautiful Moroccan design called Tealeidoscope.

'They are gorgeous, Charlotte, I'm looking forward to trying them out,' Silvia went on to tell Charlotte about how her art teacher always made a cup of tea from a different teapot after every class.

'You know what, Charlotte; we should go to the Sassafras Tea Shop. You will love it; it's up in the Dandenong Ranges. You would not believe how many different teapots, tea cups and tea leaves. Plus we could go to Miss Marples café afterwards for lunch, Phoebe and Nathaniel could come too.'

'That sounds like a fun day out, I've heard of Miss Marples but I didn't know there was a tea shop there. Let's go in the next couple of weeks.'

'I only found out about the tea shop when I saw a post on Facebook. I wonder how Facebook knows I like tea?' laughed Silvia. 'I'm sure it will be a great day out.'

'Facebook knows everything!' Charlotte laughed. 'Yeah, I'd love to go, it should be fun. I'll see when Phoebe is free and we'll make a plan.' which was something Charlotte loved to do, make plans.

'Great, I think it will be good for Phoebe to get out of the house too, don't you think?'

'For sure, it will be. I don't think she's left the house since she had Nathanial, she's such a hermit.'

After they finished their tea, Charlotte washed up and Silvia helped her fold some washing. They walked the two blocks to Acland Street to their favourite café. Charlotte ordered a chai latté and a vanilla slice which they shared and Silvia a strong flat white. The atmosphere was buzzing. The café was trendy, decorated with 60s style chairs and tables with memorabilia from the sixties and seventies covering the walls.

'Silv, I'm thinking of getting Botox. What do you think, you work in that industry?'

'Oh my God no!' Silvia exclaimed, 'you're not ever getting Botox. For a start, you don't need it, you already look fantastic,' Silvia put her hand on Charlotte's arm, leaning back as if to say what the hell are you thinking. 'And you don't know the half of what goes on at the clinic where I work.'

'Really, what do you mean?' Charlotte was interested in any inside gossip.

'Well, the other day a woman came in, she had had Botox and fillers about a month prior and she took photos of herself from day one until she came back in worried and wanting to see Claudia who is our Botox consultant. At first, her forehead looked a little red, but with each photo it changed, getting progressively worse. In one photo, her skin had blistered and gradually her skin looked as if it was rotting.'

'Oh my God, really, why? What happened?'

'Apparently she had an allergic reaction to the Botox, eventually it healed but I think she wants to claim damages, and that's not all. We've had a number of cases where women end up in hospital because of bad reactions but no one talks about it. They are too embarrassed, and don't want their friends or even their partners to know they've had it done, so they pretend they've had a medical episode.

It really makes me angry they don't show these photos to women and girls who are thinking about having it done. Bloody hell, Charlotte, you're young, why would you have Botox, of all things? There's nothing wrong with you.'

'Mmm, I've noticed a few wrinkles lately and the girl in my office has had it done, and she looks awesome.'

'She might look awesome but eventually she will age, we are all going to age Charlotte, and beauty is part of the aging process, embrace it, there's nothing wrong with aging.'

'But just because some women have bad reactions, doesn't mean all do. I think it's up to the individual. Silv, if it makes you feel better about yourself there's nothing wrong with it, in my opinion anyway. And why are you working for a plastic surgeon if you don't agree with what he does?'

'Mmm, sometimes I do wonder why I'm there but the universe has mysterious ways. Maybe these people are meant to be in my life for an unknown reason. Anyway, Charlotte, in the end it's up to you but it's not for me,' Silvia hesitated, 'not yet anyway maybe when I'm sixty, I'll change my mind,' she laughed.

Over their coffee and cake, they talked some more about Botox, fillers and plastic surgery, and then Charlotte brought up the mystery of Rita's death.

'Have you heard any more about Rita? Do you believe Frank murdered her?'

'I contacted the police last week and they said they were finalising details for the coroner. I asked the officer straight out what their line of enquiry was. Did they believe she was murdered, and he said no, in their opinion it was an accident. It's made me realise how dangerous it is to be distracted, she must have been focusing on the wood for the fire and not on how close she was to the well. Her mind must have been elsewhere. You know what, Charlotte? I'm over it, I don't bloody know what happened, and I'm not going to allow my mind to wonder or guess. I can make up any story in my head but where will it get me?'

They had tears in their eyes as Charlotte reached across and gave Silvia a hug.

'That's true Aunty, we don't know what happened and maybe we never will. It's so hard not to have closure.'

Silvia nodded, the tears trickled down her cheek and she began to look in her bag for a tissue.

Charlotte placed her napkin in Silvia's hand. 'Here Aunty use this, I'm sorry for bringing it up.'

'Don't be silly, it's been playing on my mind too, but nothing has changed.'

Charlotte looked down, not knowing what to say.

'Oh, God Charlotte, let's lighten the subject.' Silvia took Charlotte's hand and squeezed it.

Chapter 31

Silvia arrived home with all her art supplies. Nick had left a note to say he was visiting his parents and would be back before dinner. She decided to do a little more work on her portrait, it was nearly finished but she was struggling to get the smile right.

Perched on top of the couch, Molly watched her bringing in her easel and going out again to fetch the rest of her art supplies. Stretching, Molly jumped off the couch and started meowing for food.

'OK, OK, I just got home, give me a minute,' Silvia walked into her art room and laid her supplies on the table then went to the laundry. The cat's bowl had old uneaten bits of food stuck to it; she cleaned it out and put in some fresh food. The cat scratched at the scratching post before padding into the laundry to check what was on offer.

'I hope it's good enough for you,' she said, patting Molly between her ears.

She went back into her art room and pulled the cloth off her new easel. Opening it up, she rolled it closer to the window so she could see with natural light rather than having to switch the light on. She sifted through her new items, pleased with her choices, and placed them in their correct spots on the table.

Silvia picked up her nearly finished portrait and placed it on the easel standing back to admire it. She was amazed at the difference it made to view it at different angles and light. She sat down, pleased with what she had done so far. Yet something was missing, the smile did not look right. Gazing into the mirror beside the painting she jiggled around until she was in the correct position. She smiled. 'To hell with it, she wasn't in the mood! What was wrong with her?' Impatient and disappointed, she stood up and walked out of the room, closing the door behind her.

She walked into the kitchen and looked at the bottle of wine sitting on the bench. Screwing off the cap, she searched for her glass. The one she liked to drink out of was in the dishwasher and, being a wine drinker, it was all about the glass. She found another glass which was equally impressive, deep and round and tapered in at the top with a long, elegant stem. She poured the wine into the glass. Instead of drinking, she looked at it and pondered, 'Do I really feel like it?' She waited a moment or two before bringing the glass to her mouth and taking a sip. Ugh, it really did taste awful. She wondered, 'Am I on the verge of becoming an alcoholic? Drinking during the day is not a good idea.' Instead of drinking it, she tipped it out into the sink.

She walked into the room which she had set up for yoga. It was airy and light with clean white walls and warm carpet; in the middle of the room was her yoga mat and in front of the mat she had a little altar with a candle and a vase for fresh flowers. Her little yoga stool where she meditated was located at the back of the room. She sat on her stool and closed her eyes, she had been doing yoga now for many years and was used to meditating.

With her spine straight, she sat still, at first taking a few deep breaths and began to relax, but after a while it was as though something overtook her breathing. Was she the breather or was the breath breathing her? The breaths became longer and deeper, which continued for about 5 minutes and then the breathing was minimal as though she wasn't even breathing. Her head tilted back, leaving her throat exposed; it was as though something had overtaken her but she was unafraid. She stayed in that position until it felt like her neck would break so she forced it back up.

In her sitting pose, her breathing began to deepen once more, and, as if on auto pilot, she began moving her hands in mudra (hand and finger positions) her hands moved like a dance to the rhythm of her breath, something had taken over her body but she trusted that whatever was happening, it wasn't sinister. She believed she was safe and connected with love. This serene state went on for about 20 to 30 minutes before it left her. After her meditation she felt invigorated and alive as though she had just been given a spiritual cleansing. Silvia decided to keep the mystical experience to herself. It was simply incredible. During the meditation, she was guided to the understanding that it could not be taught to anyone. It was a gift of the highest order.

Chapter 32

Pat parked the car behind some shrubs about 300 metres from the rural property, and slowly walked down the long driveway towards the house. Knocking on the front door, but there was no answer. So Pat walked around to the back of the house.

Rita had been getting dinner ready but knew it would be a cold night so was bringing in some firewood; it was the only heating in the cottage. The wheelbarrow was nearly full but there was room for a couple more logs. She was about to pick up another log when she felt a presence coming towards her. Startled, she looked up and saw a figure standing there.

'Hello, can I help you?'

'I'm sorry I tried knocking but no one answered. My car ran out of petrol and I thought someone might be able to help me.'

'Do you have a phone?' Rita asked. It would be odd, perhaps even suspicious, not to have one.

'My phone's dead,' Pat held up the phone.

'You can use mine if you like. I'll just go and get it from inside,' she went to walk towards the house but Pat stood in front of her blocking her.

'What about your husband, couldn't he help me?' Pat started shaking and was becoming agitated.

Rita became afraid; she didn't want this intruder to think she wasn't married and was living alone. Frank had left two weeks ago, after an argument. He had decided it was best for him to leave. He didn't want to go back to hitting Rita because he knew it would land him in jail. Rita was sad about it but it was for the best; maybe he would sort himself out and come back to her. In a way she provoked a lot of the arguments; they both needed some time apart.

'Well, ah my husband should be home soon but in the meantime I can call you an Uber and they can take you to a service station.' Rita suggested.

Pat grabbed her arm, 'No I'm happy to wait, I'd like to meet Nick and see if he can help me.'

'Let go of me,' Rita demanded, trying to wrench her arm away, 'My husband's name isn't Nick, you must have the wrong address.'

Pat exploded, 'I saw you with him!'

Rita's mind was racing, what the fuck was this idiot on about.

'I don't know what you mean, my husband's name is Frank, let me go,' she struggled and broke free of the grip. She tore across the yard, but tripped over one of the logs which sent her sprawling onto the ground. Rita scrambled up and started running again, only to slip out of sight.

Pat stood there trying to comprehend what had happened, then cautiously walked over to the well and looked down. Rita was laying there, her eyes staring back not blinking, there was a slurry of mud and water surrounding her lifeless body. Blood trickled from her mouth.

Pat sat beside the well, in shock, waiting for Nick to come home. She had lied, he wasn't coming home, he must have been away on a business trip.

Pat took the wheelbarrow and placed it near the well, knocking it over to make it look like an accident. Pat hadn't gone there with the intention of killing her, so technically it *was* an accident.

Chapter 33

The phone rang, 'Hey Silv, looks like we picked the perfect day to go, the weather is going to be sunny and 22 degrees. We'll meet at Phoebe's at 10.30; she said she will drive because she has the baby seat.'

'Oh, OK Charlotte, so Phoebe doesn't mind driving up there?'

'Yeah, it's easier than taking out the baby seat and putting it in your car.'

'True, I'll get myself ready now and meet you there.' Silvia hung up and started on the breakfast dishes, Nick was outside mowing the lawn. She threw some washing in the machine and took a shower, blow-dried her hair and donned a pair of light blue denim jeans, a white shirt and some skin-coloured sandals.

The washing machine beeped three times. Silvia placed the washing into the basket and went outside to hang it on the line.

Nick was pottering around in the garden.

'Nick, I'm going soon,' she said as she pegged the washing onto the line.

'Where are you going again?'

'I told you, we're going to the tea shop up in the Dandenong's.'

'Oh that's right, honey, have a great day and send my love to the girls, oh and Nathanial,' he smiled showing his beautiful white teeth as he walked toward Silvia, leaning down to kiss her.

Silvia finished putting the washing on the line, 'I'll probably be home around 3 o'clock.'

'Have fun,' Nick had planned to do the gardening and later drop in to see his parents.

'We will,' Silvia chirped, turning and heading off.

He always dropped in to see them on the weekend, helping his father with the gardening or doing odd jobs. One time his mother called him to say his father was about to climb onto the roof. He wanted to clean the pergola, having spotted moss growing on it. Nick asked to speak to his Dad. He was firm and told his father, 'Under no circumstances are you to climb on the roof.' At his age, a fall could prove fatal. His father agreed to Nick's conditions but whether he would keep his word, Nick was doubtful.

Charlotte was already at Phoebe's when Silvia arrived. Phoebe was packing the car with a big bag full of nappies and bits and pieces she thought she might need. Charlotte was holding Nathanial getting ready to secure him into the baby seat.

'Hi Aunty, you can sit in the front because I want to sit next to Nathanial,' said Charlotte.

'Good, because I get sick in the back seat,' Silvia was happy to comply, 'plus I know the directions.'

Once they were all in the car, their seat belts on and buckled, Silvia directed Phoebe through the back roads towards Belgrave. They came to the roundabout just past the Puffing Billy station.

'Keep going straight, it's a steep road but it's the quickest way,' Silvia directed.

The road was very steep and winding; they all admired the forest of massive trees and the canopy of ferns above them. You could almost see fairies hiding amongst the shadows, jumping and weaving through the flickering sunlight that was filtering through the lacework of leaves and fernery.

'Aren't these trees amazing?' said Phoebe in awe.

'Mmm they are huge, but I wouldn't want to live around here. I mean could you imagine having to drive around here on a winter's day? Or in the fog? And in summer, you'd have the worry of fires,' said Charlotte.

'I know but it is beautiful, I mean for a day trip, but yeah I wouldn't feel comfortable living around here. When you get to the end of this road, turn right and it's a couple of kilometres to the town of Sassafras,' Silvia instructed.

On arrival, they parked in a small car park behind the shops. Surprisingly, it was quite busy for such a small town. It was a tourist destination which explained why there were so many people getting about.

Charlotte helped Phoebe to fasten the baby sling and Silvia helped Nathaniel into it. It was so much easier for her to manoeuvre through the shops than with a pram. Nathanial liked to be close to his mother and slept most of the time.

'If we want to go to Miss Marples for lunch, we will have to wait in a queue because they don't take bookings. Let's just browse through the shops first, it's too early to eat,' said Silvia.

'Can we look at the tea shop first?' Charlotte requested.

From the front, the tea shop looked tiny but first impressions were deceiving. The sign above its entrance read:-

tealeaves
the crazy teapot shop!

Within the confines of the shop was an Aladdin's cave. It had a magical effect with all the colours and quirkiness of the teapots and cups. There were shelves with so many varieties of teas and they also sold coffee and chocolates.

They spent about an hour looking through the tea shop. Silvia was interested in the tea leaves and the various concoctions like teas suitable for cleansing, energy, and sleep. Phoebe and Charlotte were more interested in exploring the nooks and crannies hiding little objects like tea spoons, tea towels and cups and saucers.

'Look at these cute mugs,' Phoebe pointed to a collection of Marini Ferlazzo Wild Planet mugs.

'Oh how gorgeous, are they otters?' Charlotte picked up one of the mugs; it had two cute otters surrounded by flowers. 'They are otters, how sweet,' she answered herself.

'Look at this cute elephant mug; I'm going to buy the set! They are just so funny and would make anyone happy,' said Phoebe.

'I'm going to buy them for you,' Charlotte announced.

'Don't be silly, Charlotte, I can buy them for myself.'

'But I want to, besides you shouted me to the movies last time, so I want to buy these for you.'

'Aww, thank you.'

After choosing what they wanted, they left feeling satisfied with their purchases. Silvia had bought some organic cleansing tea, Charlotte bought Phoebe the set of Wild Planet mugs, along with a Moroccan Tealeidoscope tea pot to match her cups.

'Let's put these in the car and then we're off to lunch at Miss Marples,' said Silvia.

They made their way to the car, passing a little shop that sold angora shawls.

'Oh, I'm just going to have a quick look in here,' said Silvia. 'I've wanted a shawl for ages.'

The girls waited outside, they had no intention of buying a shawl, or anything from that shop, angora or merino wool was way too expensive. A few minutes later Silvia emerged holding a bag with a mustard-coloured possum/merino shawl which she pulled it out to show them.

'Oh, it's beautiful, you'll get a lot of wear out of it,' said Charlotte.

'I love the colour,' said Phoebe.

'It was expensive but I love it! As I said I've wanted one for ages,' Silvia reassured herself and Charlotte and Phoebe that she deserved it.

After putting their purchases in the car, they walked to Miss Marples and waited outside.

They didn't have to wait long. A woman wearing an old-fashioned dress with an apron over it directed them to a cosy corner.

The décor and atmosphere was set in the 1950s. Anyone who read Agatha Christie novels or watched the movies made from her murder mysteries would know that Miss Marples was one of her main characters. The walls of the tea room were decorated with pictures of Miss Marples in various movie scenes.

Silvia remembered watching the movie 'Murder She Said,' where Miss Marples reports witnessing a murder through the window of a passing train. The police find no evidence of the crime and it is up to Miss Marples to uncover the truth, taking on the role of a private detective. Margaret Rutherford played the character and was one of the best actresses for the part, in Silvia's opinion.

They ordered tea, scones and sandwiches. Nathanial woke once the food arrived so Phoebe breast fed him while she sipped her tea.

'I love it up here in the Dandenong Ranges, we should come here more often. I feel like I'm in another world,' Phoebe proclaimed.

'Yeah, I do too,' Charlotte agreed, 'there's something about the forest and all the trees and even the shops here that make me feel, I don't know, happy.'

Silvia and her two nieces enjoyed each other's company, talking and laughing all through lunch.

She would take no argument from them as Silvia insisted on paying for their lunch. As they were leaving, her phone rang; a number she didn't recognize came up. Silvia gestured for Phoebe and Charlotte to meet her back at the car while she answered the call.

It was Rita's father, 'Hello Silvia, I have some news for you,' Silvia immediately recognised his voice. 'I'm sorry, excuse my manners, how have you been?'

'Don't be sorry, I'm fine,' Silvia paused.

'Yes, well as I said I have some news for you, a detective called me this morning and said they are going to reopen the case,' he paused for a moment.

Silvia listened and nodded but she could not comprehend the information she was hearing.

'The detective said they had received a call from one of Rita's neighbours. She recalled that on her way home from work she saw a person walking towards a car that was parked in a suspicious position behind some shrubs, not too far from Rita's house.' He paused for a moment then continued. 'It was a few days before— before you know, you and Ted found her,' the words were understandably very difficult for him to say. 'The neighbour thought it was odd at the time, but she didn't think it had anything to do with what happened to Rita,' he cleared his throat and continued. 'The detective said that it had been playing on her mind and she thought it best to tell them about what she saw.'

'And the detectives believe it's enough to reopen the case?' asked Silvia.

'They may have some other leads, I'm not sure, but I wanted to let you know.'

'Yes, thank you.' Silvia sighed.

****

Sharon finished her shift at the local supermarket. Her feet were aching and she was thankful to be going home to a cooked meal. It was around 5.15p.m. and was just starting to get dark. Pete was a good cook; he knew Sharon would be looking forward to a hearty meal after standing on her feet all day at the checkout and putting up with difficult customers. He made a roast lamb with all the trimmings, potatoes and peas with mint sauce and roast pumpkin.

She slid into her car and turned the music up. Elvis was singing 'Love Me Tender,' oh how she loved Elvis. She sang along 'tell me you are mine, I'll be yours through all the years, till the end of time.'

She turned into her street and saw someone walking along the road up ahead. She couldn't make out if it was a male or female. All the properties around there were rural so it was strange that someone would be walking along the road. As she approached, she spotted a car behind some shrubs. She turned back to see if she could recognise the person but couldn't distinguish anything because her windows had fogged up. She turned into her driveway and looked back as the car was being driven away.

'Hun, I'm home,' called Sharon, 'dinner smells delicious.' Pete had a glass of wine waiting for Sharon on the side table next to the sofa.

'Dinner will be in half an hour.'

Sharon took off her shoes and quickly visited the loo. She sat on the sofa, sipping her wine, eager to watch the last of 'Who Wants To Be a Millionaire.' Pete joined her with a can of beer in hand and a tea towel draped over his shoulder.

'Darl, I just saw someone walking down the road and get into a car that was parked behind the bushes near Rita's house,' said Sharon, keeping her gaze locked on the television.

'Strange,' replied Peter.

Which of these U.S. Presidents appeared on the television series Laugh In was it:-
 A) Lyndon Johnson - B) Richard Nixon -
C) Jimmy Carter or - D) Gerald Ford.

'B) Richard Nixon!' yelled Sharon.

****

'Constable Fredrick here, how can I help you?'

The phone was silent.

'Hello, how can I help you?'

'The, the girl they found in the well, it was an accident. I, I didn't mean it.'

'Hello, if you give me your details then I'm sure I can help you.'

The caller went silent.

'Hello, please stay on the line.'

'It was an accident, I didn't throw her into the well, I didn't go there to kill her. She tripped and fell.'

Then the phone clicked and there was silence.

Pat stared at the phone, feeling the first tinges of another migraine.

Chapter 34

Startled, she woke up to the sound of her own snoring, and turned over. Her head was pounding and her tongue felt like sandpaper stuck to the roof of her mouth. Jim was lying next to her snoring softly. The blinds were open and sunlight was streaming into the room. Sally tried opening her eyes but they didn't want to comply. Slowly she began to wake up and remember where she was.

Oh God, what a night, they were at their holiday house in Byron Bay. She was getting too old for this, she couldn't drink like she used to. She lay there feeling angry at herself for overdoing it. Taking painkillers for her hip and mixing them with liberal quantities of champagne and wine. It was – she was - absolutely stupid.

She swung her legs out of bed and softly stepped to the ensuite. She was dying for a pee and a drink of water. Standing at the sink, she gulped down one glass after another to quench her thirst and lubricate her mouth. Walking back to the bed, she admired their beautiful tropical view. The sun was shining through the palm trees and the spreading bird of paradise plants. She could hear birds chirping outside and the hum of the spa. It was going to be a glorious day. But had she ruined it already by feeling so wretched and hung over?

Jim stirred and stretched out his body, 'Could you get me a glass of water, darling?'

'Sure,' Sally replied, returning to the bathroom. As she handed him the water, she asked 'How's your head?'

'It's not too bad, nothing that a couple of Panadol won't fix. What about you? I saw you downing those flutes of champagne like they were water?'

'I know, hell, why did I open that last bottle? I wonder how Pam and Tony are feeling.'

'I'd say pretty much the same as us,' Jim rolled over and put the empty glass on the side table. He turned back and gently pulled Sally towards him, holding her close as they both fell back to sleep.

Jim woke to the smell of bacon, 'Wake up, darling, Pam and Tony are making breakfast.'

Sally woke up begrudgingly. In the ensuite, she turned on the shower and stood there soaking in the water, allowing it to wake her up. Jim joined her lathering up soap and washing her back, then she returned the favour. Jim had a hard on, he turned around taking Sally's hand and placed it on his cock. She stroked it a few times, then turned around and guided him into her from behind. After a few thrusts it was over.

Feeling a little better after the refreshing shower, Sally got out first, dressed herself and waited for Jim.

'Good morning, lovelies,' was Pam's greeting as Jim and Sally walked into the kitchen. 'How are you feeling, Sally? God, you were funny last night.'

'What do you mean?' but Sally didn't want to hear it. If she couldn't remember it, she didn't want to be reminded.

'Don't you remember, when you were in the spa, you started singing 'Happy Birthday Mr President' like Marilyn Munroe, and the next minute you were choking on a peanut. We thought you were going to die, but you coughed it up and asked for another champagne.'

'Oh God,' Sally cringed and tried to change the subject, 'That bacon smells delicious; I need a big breakfast to soak up the alcohol.'

Tony had set the table and made everyone a coffee. He felt comfortable staying at Jim and Sally's holiday house; he and Pam often spent time there with them. Jim had asked them to join them for the weekend as Sally's 50th was only a few weeks away. He wanted to go to Byron Bay to get Sally's mind off all the organising she had been doing.

'It was funny,' said Tony as he lay out the cutlery.

Jim placed two Panadol and a glass of water beside Sally, who was sitting at the dining table; she wasn't looking at all well. He went to help Pam butter the toast while she dished out the eggs and bacon.

They sat around the table and laughed about their crazy night. After finishing their breakfast, Jim suggested they go for a walk on the beach.

There was a track of about 300 metres leading from the beach house down to the beach. The sand was white and clean and the air was fresh, it seemed like summer had already arrived although it was still spring. Jim and Tony were walking ahead talking about properties and the share market. Sally and Pam followed in their tracks, talking about Sally's big party.

'Have you got everything organised?' Pam enquired.

'Yeah, everything is in place. At one point, I never thought I'd get it finished. It took lots of visits and phone calls to sort out the food and drinks we wanted, plus the music and invitations, but yeah it's all sorted now. It should be a great night.'

'So are you still going to wear that orange dress?'

'No, I've decided on something else but I want it to be a surprise,' laughed Sally. She had bought a beautiful orange dress months earlier, but it was a woman's prerogative to change her mind.

'Fair enough, I love the kaftan you're wearing now, where did you get it from?'

'I got this one from Dubai, isn't it beautiful?'

'I do love the burnt orange,' Pam enthused.

Sally's kaftan was absolutely stunning, the light picking out the orange and gold threads woven into the luxurious fabric and the brass beads along the neckline and sleeves. Sally had bought it on a stopover when she travelled to London to visit Chelsea last summer.

'There's a great shop here that sells them. Later, when we go to the market, we will stop at the shops and I'll introduce you to Ester, she has a great range.'

They walked along the sandy beach to the sound of the waves gently rolling in.

Jim stopped and turned to Sally and Pam, 'Tony and I are going to play a round of golf this afternoon, and meet up with some of the locals for a drink at the golf club.'

'Yes dear, I already gathered that,' Sally was laughing.

Jim turned back to Tony and they kept walking ahead, deep in conversation.

'You know what, Sally, I feel like jumping in,' Pam pointed to the sea.

'Are you crazy, it will be freezing?'

'No it won't, it'll be refreshing, come on,' Pam tried to persuade Sally, but she wouldn't have a bar of it.

'I haven't got my bathers.'

'I'm going in my bra and undies,' Pam took off her clothes, threw them in a pile on the sand, and she ran towards the sea laughing. Once she was waist deep, she screamed. 'God, it's cold,' she laughed.

'You're crazy,' Sally shouted, 'I'm not going to follow you.'

On hearing Pam's laughter and screaming, Jim and Tony turned to see what the commotion was about. Of course, they too plunged into the sea. Sally would have liked to jump in too but couldn't be bothered. She was still recovering from the night before, and didn't fancy getting cold and wet. Besides, she had just showered.

They didn't stay in long because the water really was freezing. No one had a towel to dry themselves off, so they patted themselves down with their clothes, throwing them back on their wet skin. They hurried back to the house.

After lounging around the house for most of the morning, Sally and Pam went shopping, dropping in to the market first. It had a wonderful atmosphere with music and the smell of exotic foods and incense. They browsed many different stalls from tie-dyed hippy clothes and candles to leather wear and art work. They enjoyed the market but Sally preferred high quality, expensive things. They walked to the local shops and browsed through the designer stores.

'Ester's shop is in this little arcade,' Sally gestured up ahead and to the left.

They made their way through the arcade to a quaint little shop. An enticing scent of bergamot and lemongrass wafted through the air from the lit soy candle on the counter top.

Racks of kaftans, tops and dresses were arranged to the left and right as Sally and Pam strolled into the shop. The clothes were arranged from lighter to darker colours. Various candles and hand creams were neatly displayed on a table in the centre of the shop. Ester also carried stock of exclusive jewellery and sandals.

Ester was sitting behind the counter reading a book. She had natural grey hair and was wearing one of her kaftans. Her skin showed the signs of having spent many hours in the sun and the sea. She was deeply tanned, her leathery skin was dotted with many sun spots. She would have been quite attractive in her youth; she looked up and smiled a greeting.

'Can I help you lovely ladies?'

'Hi Ester, it's me, Sally.'

'Oh Sally, I haven't seen you for ages.'

'I've been busy with our business and haven't had the chance to come to Byron. This is my friend, Pam, I wanted to show her your range of kaftans.'

'By all means, of course,' Ester came out from behind the counter. She was wearing a kaftan in a natural cream colour with golden embroidered leaves scattered across the fabric.

'A new range has just come in, have a look at this beautiful one.' With a sweeping motion, Ester unfurled a rich-looking deep green kaftan with red velvet ties in front of Pam.

Ester declared, 'It's quite extravagant, don't you think?'

'Not sure that I'm so extravagant,' Pam replied, laughing.

After trying on a variety of tops and hippy pants, Pam bought a beautiful sky-blue kaftan shot through with glittering silver thread. Sally bought a new pair of leather sandals and a Florian Beck designer bracelet.

'I've had enough of walking around and shopping for now, let's have some afternoon tea and rest our legs,' Pam suggested.

'Sounds good to me, my feet are swelling up,' replied Sally, 'Can you recommend a café, Ester?'

Ester suggested a local café 'with the best coffee in Byron.' They only had to walk to the end of the arcade. She wrapped their goodies and packed them into carry bags with her logo stamped on the side, Ester's Extravaganza.

Once they were seated, they sighed in unison, relieved to be off their feet. They decided on an avocado and chicken wrap each and a cappuccino. They began discussing the practice.

'I'm not sure Silvia is fitting in,' Pam stated.

'How do you mean?' Sally leaned forward, curious to hear what Pam had to say.

'Don't get me wrong, she seems to be a good person, it's just some of the comments she's made lately. Like the other day a young girl came in for Botox, and Silvia had commented, 'Why would she need it, she's so young?' 'She didn't say it to the girl but she said it to me.'

'Oh really, mmm, just keep an eye on her. Obviously if it continues, I'll have a chat with her.'

'As I said, she's nice, but it's not a good vibe if she's judging our clients.'

'I know what you mean, she's a little odd but she's reliable and naturally attractive. I think she's perfect for the front desk,' Sally paused, as their coffees were served, 'It would be a pity, but if she doesn't agree with what we do, she is a hypocrite for wanting to work with us. Keep me updated about it. Actually, Katy also mentioned a few things to me about Silvia.'

'Really, what did she say?' Pam pulled her chair closer, her eyes wide with intrigue.

'She told me Silvia was spending too much time on personal calls rather than concentrating on her work and that her mind seemed to be somewhere else.'

'Mmm, you don't know what goes on in people's lives; she doesn't talk much about her personal life.'

'Pam, I don't really care about her personal life.' Sally's palm came down on to the small table, cups and cutlery jangling, 'You know that our practice has to employ the right kind of staff, people who are happy to be promoting us. We are a tight team and can't afford any problems or negativity. If Jim hears anything about it, she'll be gone. For now I'd like you to keep an eye on her over the next few weeks. Claudia said some of her creams have gone on walkabout too. I'm not saying Silvia has stolen them but I can't imagine anyone else, can you?'

'Sally, you can't blame her with no evidence. I don't think she would have taken any product. Could it have been the cleaners?'

'I'm not blaming her, but she is the new girl and we haven't had any problems before now. I don't want to let her go, let's give her more time and see how she goes.'

The conversation changed to Katy's marriage, then Pam questioned Sally about the conversation they had after Sally's surgery, 'So, do you still think Jim's having an affair?'

'No,' Sally tried to laugh it off; she wished she'd never brought it up in the first place. 'I think I was being slightly paranoid, I wasn't feeling good within myself after the surgery.' Sally still had doubts but didn't want to say anything; she wanted to believe her doubts were just her own insecurities. 'I did think about your suggestion to have Bella pop in unexpectedly, but, no, it's all good.'

'That's good; I couldn't imagine Jim having an affair, he has too much respect for you.' Pam said in a tone that was final.

They returned to the house and chilled out, waiting for Jim and Tony to come back from golf. Pam picked up the book she had been reading for the past month and Sally flicked through the latest Vogue magazine.

'Liam, how are you?' Sally was delighted to be interrupted by a call from her son.

'Yeah I'm good, Mum, I called to ask, if it's OK for me to invite Keith and his girlfriend to your 50th?'

'Of course it is. I didn't know Keith had a girlfriend. It will be good to see him again, plus it will be nice to meet his girlfriend.'

'Thanks Mum, how have you been anyway?'

'I've been busy organising my birthday. We're in Byron at the moment with Pam and Tony.'

'Oh, say hi to Pam for me.'

'I will. While I have you on the phone, do you know how to set up a surveillance system, something simple?'

'I thought you had a surveillance system?'

'No, I'm not talking about at home. Some of our products have gone missing and we suspect it may be an employee. I would like a simple camera set up in our supply room.'

'Really! Yeah I can do that for you, easy. Next time I'm down, I'll swing by the clinic. I've got to go, Mum, another call is coming in.'

'Thanks Liam, bye love.'

When Jim and Tony returned, Sally made up a large cheese platter with truffle cheese, goat's cheese, hot and mild salami, a variety of dips and some crusty bread. They sat on the deck and Jim opened a bottle of Cloudy Bay Sauvignon Blanc, pouring them all a glass.

'Did you call to make the reservations for dinner, Jim?' asked Sally.

'Yep, I certainly did, at Beach Byron for 7.30.'

'Great, I was worried that they might not have a table,' replied Sally.

'When is Chelsea coming home?' asked Pam, turning to Jim.

'She's back a week before Sally's birthday and staying for five weeks. It'll be great having her home,' replied Jim.

'I can't wait to see her, I mean we face-time often but I can't wait to see her in the flesh and just spend time with her. Plus she wants to catch up with her friends, of course,' said Sally.

'You won't know yourself, with your 50th coming up and Chelsea home. Cheers to you, Sally,' Pam held up her glass and they all clicked glasses.

Chapter 35

Nick was watching the cricket while Silvia was in her art room painting. An ad came on so Nick flicked though his junk mail to check if there was anything he had missed before deleting them. There was the normal rubbish, JB Hi-Fi Hottest Deals, Everyday Rewards, Qantas Hotel Deals, RACV Top Selling Cars. Something caught Nick's eye, a name he didn't recognize - Ennis Kerry with the subject line:-

I'M SORRY ABOUT YOUR WIFE.

Silvia sat in her art room, her portrait was almost finished; as it was her first portrait, she never imagined it would be so difficult. She was happy with the eyes, almost everyone had told her the eyes are the hardest, but Silvia disagreed, for her the difficult part was getting her smile right. Was it the angle of the mouth, or was it the eyes that held the smile, she pondered as she painted.

Nick felt a wave of confusion, he opened the email and there was no content. Was it a threat of some kind? What the hell was this email about, was it some kind of sick joke? Who was Ennis Kerry?

Nick googled the name Enniskerry and what came up made him feel sick to the stomach, Ennis Kerry:- Village in the Republic of Ireland. That can't be right, so he googled just the name Ennis – again what came up was disturbing, Ennis:- Town in the Republic of Ireland.

'Hey honey, would you like a coffee?' Silvia stood in the doorway of the living room.

Nick flicked his phone off and placed it beside him on the couch. 'Thanks I'd love one. Have you finished your painting?'

Silvia walked into the kitchen, 'No, I can't get the smile right, so I've decided to put it away for a couple of weeks until I feel motivated again.' Silvia took out the coffee percolator and put in some fresh ground beans, and placed some carrot and walnut cake she had made the previous night onto a plate.

The cricket was on the television screen but Nick wasn't paying attention. He was thinking about the mysterious email. Was it someone who knew Sean, maybe a family member or a friend? Were they threatening Nick that something was going to happen to Silvia? "I'M SORRY ABOUT YOUR WIFE."

'There you go,' Silvia walked back into the living room carrying a tray with the coffee and cake. She placed it on the coffee table, 'What are the scores?'

'I'm not sure, I haven't been paying attention,' Nick replied in a daze.

Silvia continued, oblivious to his disinterested reply, 'I forgot to tell you, yesterday, Melissa was called in for a meeting with Jim and Sally. They were talking for ages, and when she came out, her eyes were red. I think she was crying.'

'Really, I wonder why?' Nick tried to sound interested.

'I think I know,' Silvia sipped her coffee and broke off a piece of cake. 'Judith, you know the nurse who I like?'

Nick nodded.

Silvia continued, excited to reveal her inside knowledge, 'She told me that Sally had a hidden camera installed in Claudia's room. I have a sneaky hunch it has something to do with that, apparently someone has been stealing cosmetics.' Silvia waited for Nick to respond.

Nick's mind was elsewhere. He gave a grunt, taking a long swig of coffee.

'If it was Melissa, I doubt they would sack her, I think they would probably just caution her. I mean, I don't know if I'm right, but if anyone had the opportunity to steal, it would be her. She's at the clinic alone a lot of the time,' Silvia concluded.

In a serious tone Nick changed the subject, 'Silvia, I went through my junk mail and there was a strange email. Here, take a look,' he passed her his phone.

Chapter 36

The big day had arrived, now everyone could show off how good they looked. The women were wearing the most extravagant gowns and jewellery and, of course, their hair and makeup had to be perfect. As for the men, they were dressed in their finest suits, not to mention their watches. Not any watch would do, it had to be the perfect showpiece. A Rolex was out of the reach of many but a Breitling, a Tag Heuer, an Omega or Nixon would fit the bill.

Silvia and Nick had booked a hotel room for the big night. They wanted to enjoy the whole experience of going to The Dome and mingling with all the interesting guests who had accepted an invitation to Sally's 50th birthday party. The hotel they were staying at was literally a two minute walk to the venue.

Silvia looked effortlessly beautiful. She wore a dusty pale pink dress that hugged her body. It had silver flowers swirled through the fabric and she paired it with silver stilettos. She tied her hair back in a low pony tail and clasped a few stray strands with a silver clip. Her skin was lightly-tanned; she wore dark pink lipstick with minimal eye shadow. Nick looked just as stylish and they made an eye-catching couple. He chose a navy blue suit but didn't wear a watch. He was not comfortable wearing any kind of jewellery, not even his wedding ring, although he did wear it on special occasions.

They arrived at the hotel early enough to have a relaxed sex session before getting ready. Sex was important to both of them especially before a big night out; it kept them close. The cryptic email was still on their minds but they didn't know if it should be taken seriously. It could have been spam, so they dismissed it and decided to wait and see if they received any further contact.

'Let's get going Silvia, have you got everything?'

'Yes, I'm nearly ready,' Silvia sprayed her perfume into the air and walked through it. 'Oh can you grab Sally's present, I left it in the suitcase?'

Nick started hunting through the suitcase and pulled out a little package wrapped in gold paper, it was tied with gold and silver ribbon with a small birthday card tucked under the bow.

'I hope she likes them,' said Silvia.

'She had better like them,' laughed Nick 'and if she doesn't, she can just re-gift them.'

'Exactly,' said Silvia, grabbing her clutch purse as they walked out the door.

They had bought Sally a pair of white gold diamond drop earrings. They weren't extravagantly expensive but were enough to cover the cost of the evening's function.

When they reached the entrance to The Dome, they were directed to a private function room. Silvia was taken aback with the beauty of the place. The intricate details in the tiled mosaic floor were amazing and the ceiling was even more breathtaking. The Dome was modelled on the Duomo Cathedral in Florence, which she and Nick had visited three years ago.

Silvia turned to look at Nick, 'What an amazing place, Nick, isn't it beautiful? Look at the stained glass arched windows,' she whispered.

'Pretty impressive,' said Nick who, with his arm around her waist, drew Silvia closer to him.

A waiter walked over to them with a selection of champagne, crown lager or sparkling water, with thin slices of lime placed on the side. Silvia took a champagne and Nick a lager.

'There's Pam,' said Silvia as she took Nick's hand and walked over to introduce him.
Was Pam already a bit tipsy? She was certainly louder than her usual loud self, calling out, 'Silvia, you made it!'

'Yes,' they hugged and air kissed, 'This is Nick, my husband.'

'Nice to meet you, Nick. This is my friend Tony,' she turned to Tony who was a large kind-looking man with a greying beard and friendly blue eyes.

They shook hands and talked about how grand the venue was. Another waiter walked over to them with a selection of hors d'oeuvres, smoked salmon crostini, chorizo and prawn skewers and Thai chicken satay with peanut sauce, napkins on hand.

Silvia took a salmon crostini, Nick a chorizo and prawn skewer and Pam and Tony the Thai Chicken.

Pam looked lovely with her red hair up in a twisted bun. She was wearing a dark green silk dress with a lacy green and red shawl draped over her shoulders. Tony looked a little out of place wearing a black suit and a cream shirt that was too tight for his stomach.

'Have you seen Sally?' asked Silvia.

'Oh my God, she looks gorgeous! Haven't you seen her yet? She was over by the door greeting people, you must have missed her.'

'Oh, OK,' and catching Nick's eye, she said, 'Let's make our way over there now, Nick.' To Pam and Tony, Silvia said, 'Must see the birthday girl! We'll catch you later.'

They walked towards the door and Silvia caught sight of Sally. She had her hair up in a messy bun and was wearing a black satin jump suit with a silver belt and diamond necklace. Sally looked stunning. Her lips were painted burnt orange and she had a burnt orange clip holding her hair in place. Jim was standing beside her greeting the guests when he noticed Silvia, 'Hello, lovely,' he turned to Sally, 'Look who's here,' and gestured to Silvia.

Sally swung around, her arms in the air, 'Hey, Silvia you look beautiful, I love your dress.'

After Sally found out it was Melissa, who had been steeling their products, she felt bad that she had judged Silvia. Melissa was so embarrassed and explained that she had problems at home. It was no excuse for steeling, although she put on a sob story and begged Jim and Sally to forgive her and give her another chance.

'Thank you, Sally but it's you who looks stunning. Pam said you looked gorgeous, but really you look better than gorgeous,' laughed Silvia. 'This is Nick, my husband.'

Nick gave Sally a kiss on each cheek, something he was accustomed to being Greek, and shook Jim's hand.

'Oh before I forget, this is for you,' Silvia handed Sally the present.

'Thank you, that's very kind of you. I hope you enjoy your night; it should be fun,' Sally kissed Silvia. As more guests arrived, Sally was distracted. Jim turned to talk to other guests. Nick and Silvia decided to see if they could find Melissa, or any of the other girls Silvia worked with.

The venue was filling up and the noise of all the conversations was getting louder and louder. There was a piano playing somewhere in the background, the champagne was flowing, people were laughing and more food was being passed around by the waiters.

'Hey, Silvia, come over here and join us,' Silvia turned to see Claudia gesturing to her; she was with Katy and some other people Silvia didn't know. Holding Nick's hand, they walked over to the group and to many more introductions. Lots more air kissing and small talk about the incredible venue.

Everything in the room shifted as the music changed to upbeat dancing music. A few people started to dance. The next minute they saw Pam busting into a move on the dance floor, she was hilarious, doing the dance that Elaine did on one of Jerry Seinfeld's episodes. Pam was clearly mimicking her, and the guests watched on, laughing.

More waiters came over with trays of margaritas this time. You couldn't fault the food and drinks which were flowing nonstop. The waiting staff passed around trays of mini burgers of chicken, beef and lamb, calamari rings and potato rosti.

Nick and Silvia mingled with the guests and danced to a few songs until Silvia had to sit down because her feet were killing her.

'Nick, my feet are aching, I'm going to sit down for a while.'

'Do you want me to come with you?'

'No, you mingle.'

They gave each other a quick kiss and Silvia walked off the dance floor to find somewhere to rest. Sitting alone at a table, she watched everyone, her feet a little swollen. She was wearing new shoes that looked beautiful with her dress. If only she had known how terribly uncomfortable they would be. She took them off and rubbed her feet.

Nick was talking to Claudia's husband and Claudia was dancing with Sally and a group of other women. Someone came up behind her and whispered in her ear, 'You're looking lovely tonight,' in a provocative way.

Silvia turned to see Jim standing there, 'Thank you, Jim,' she replied blushing.

'Is that Angel you're wearing?' he handed her a margarita.

'Yes it is, how did you know?' Silvia was feeling the effects of the alcohol and really didn't need another drink but she accepted the margarita from him.

'I know my perfumes, it's very sexy, Silvia,' he gave her a mischievous look.

In that moment she realised he was flirting with her big time. She was self-conscious and a little embarrassed although she liked the attention.

'How are you enjoying the night?'

'Apart from my feet aching from these shoes, I'm having a ball, maybe too much fun. I'm feeling a bit tipsy,' replied Silvia.

'Believe me, there are a lot of people here tonight who've had a few too many, and you're not one of them,' said Jim, as he sat next to her he rubbed his hand on her thigh.

'Ah, thank you Jim, that's good to know,' Silvia didn't want to make a fool of herself. She had seen other women drink too much, and it was not pretty. She wanted to tell him to remove his hand but didn't want to make a scene.

At that moment, a distinguished looking gentleman interrupted them. 'There you are, Jim, I've been looking all over for you. I was speaking to your lovely wife earlier but haven't caught up with you.'

Jim quickly moved away from Silvia, stood up and shook his hand, then he turned to Silvia, 'Silvia, this is David; he's one of the anaesthetists who works with me in theatre.'

'Nice to meet you, David,' said Silvia, glad for the interruption.

'Silvia is one of my girls; she works for me at the clinic.'

'Lovely to meet you, Silvia,' said David, then turned to Jim and they started talking. It was Silvia's chance to get up and excuse herself, saying she had promised Melissa to dance with her to the next song.

She felt relieved as she didn't find it easy talking to Jim. He had flirted with her at work but she had never taken it seriously, but lately whenever their eyes would meet they would linger a little longer than necessary. There was chemistry between them but Silvia understood it was his power she liked, not him. She was very in tune with her feelings and would never cheat on Nick, nor would she cheat with another woman's husband, although she liked to be admired.

Even though she loved Nick with all her heart, deep down she saw him as powerless because he had never taken ownership of what he had done all those years ago. In a way she saw him as weak and perhaps she saw herself as weak and that's why she admired Jim. He seemed to be what Nick wasn't: powerful and charismatic.

Silvia walked through the happy throng of people looking for Melissa. She saw Nick through the crowd and waved to him. All of a sudden, the music stopped and there was the loud clinking of a glass.

'Quiet everyone, quiet; let's get the birthday girl up here. Come on up, Sally, and you too, Jim,' announced one of Sally's family members, 'it's time for the speeches.'

Sally made her way to the podium, Jim shook David's hand, 'Duty is calling,' he said, grinning as he made his way through the crowd.

Eventually the room quietened down. Silvia walked over to Nick who put his arm around her waist. They craned their necks to try and spot Sally through the crowd.

Sally stood on a small platform next to the piano with Jim by her side so everyone could see them.

'That must be Sally's sister,' Silvia whispered to Nick. The woman who had been clinking the glass looked very similar to Sally although she looked older, perhaps because she hadn't had as much plastic surgery as Sally.

The speeches didn't go on for too long. One of her friends got up onto the podium and spoke about growing up together and being friends through thick and thin, telling everyone about some of the mischief they had made in their youth, and everyone began to laugh. Then Jim had his turn, telling Sally how lovely she looked tonight and announcing his gift of the trip to Paris after the Christmas break which he'd had great difficulty to keep a secret from her. All the guests applauded and cheered.

Sally was shocked but managed to hold back her emotions. She hugged Jim, saying 'thank you' over and over. It was Sally's turn. She thanked everyone for their well wishes and gifts and spoke about how proud she was of Liam her son and how happy she was to have Chelsea home. She went on to say something Silvia found strange: she thanked Jim for choosing her as his bride all those years ago. Why would she thank him? Didn't she have enough self-esteem to believe he should be thanking her? But that was Silvia trying to analyse everything.

After the speeches, the music started up again and the dancing was getting funnier. There were groups of people dancing in a conga line, weaving in and out of the tables, to which Nick and Tony had joined in. It must have been all those margaritas flowing, Silvia thought. She and Melissa danced to a couple of songs before Silvia yelled into Melissa's ear, 'I need to pee, do you know where the ladies is?'

Melissa pointed her in the direction, 'It's through the arched doorway, you can't miss it.'

'Thanks, do you need to go?'

'No, I went before we started dancing,' said Melissa turning to dance with some of the other women on the dance floor.

Feeling the effects of the alcohol kicking in, Silvia headed for the arched doorway.

****

In the ladies rest room, Sally was sitting on the toilet. She overheard some women talking about one of the surgeons having an affair with one of the nurses. They were saying she wasn't even attractive and they didn't understand what he saw in her. They must have realised someone was in one of the cubicles and began to whisper and giggle as they walked out.

Sally didn't recognise any of their voices, but was sure she heard Jim's name being mentioned. Anger built up inside of her. She thought how easy it was to hear all the gossip just by being in the lavatory, especially when women had too much to drink. They spoke loudly and didn't think about who may be listening. Stupid bitches, she thought.

****

Was that what she thought she saw? Silvia was about to open the female restroom door, when out of the corner of her eye, she saw Jim in the mirror with another man. Who was it?

She turned to get a better look; at the end of the corridor there was a mirror reflecting the men's lavatory door. The mirror was placed in that position to direct men to the correct place. Reflected in the mirror, you could see the sign Gentlemen's Rest Room, which was just around the corner from the Ladies Rest Room.

Silvia's mind took a while to catch up with her eyes; was Jim grabbing that man's crotch and kissing him on the mouth? Was that Bob who she had met at the clinic on a couple of occasions? She kept looking, and saw Bob mouthing the word 'later' to Jim. Bob turned to walk in her direction as Jim turned to walk into the Gentlemen's lavatory. Silvia moved her head so Bob couldn't see she had been watching them. Her mind was trying to process what she had witnessed. Does Jim swing both ways? The thought made her chuckle inwardly, but she felt a little sorry for Sally.

****

After washing her hands, Sally applied some fresh lipstick, she was about to walk out of the ladies when Silvia burst in. They bumped into each other and Sally's handbag fell, and all her belongings were sprawled over the floor.

'Oh, I'm so sorry, Sally, let me help you,' said Silvia who was a little drunk.

'It's fine, don't worry, Sally reassured her, 'it's really not your fault.' Sally's mind was still on those bitches gossiping about the surgeon having an affair. She was planning to confront Jim.

Crouching down, they picked up Sally's things: a lipstick, a set of keys, mascara, some perfume. Silvia picked up a laminated card which she showed to Sally, asking 'Where, where did you get this from?'

Chapter 37

Her heart racing, she opened her eyes, a tinny pinhole of light shone through the darkness.

'Help me,' she screamed, 'help me, help me!!!'

Was she in a coffin? Who had placed her there? She couldn't breath, she was suffocating.

Memories came flooding back. She was in Sally and Jim's suite.

****

Silvia burst into the ladies, she bumped into Sally and her handbag fell, all her belongings were sprawled over the floor.

'Oh, I'm so sorry, Sally, let me help you.'

'It's fine, don't worry, Sally reassured her, 'it's really not your fault.'

Crouching down, they picked up Sally's things: a lipstick, a set of keys, mascara, some perfume. Silvia picked up a laminated card which she showed to Sally, asking 'Where, where did you get this from?'

'Oh that,' she took the card from Silvia's hand. 'My brother's partner, Pat, gave it to me. Well, we call him Pat but his real name is Sean. Being Irish and born on St Patrick's Day, the name Pat stuck, and it's easier to talk about Pat than to call him Sean. It stops people questioning me about my brother being gay. These days everyone accepts gay couples, but not so much twenty years ago.'

Silvia's mind went into a whirlwind, swirling around from the alcohol and from what she had just seen and heard. She knew Sally had a brother and his partner's name was Pat, but she had assumed Pat was short for Patricia.

Silvia was stunned and felt sick as she listened. What was she hearing? It couldn't be - no, this was not happening.

'They've been together for around twenty years now. You know about the luck of the Irish and four leaf clovers. He fell off a cliff and survived so that's pretty lucky, I'd say. I mean, he gets lots of migraines from the fall but he survived, you've heard of The Gap, haven't you?'

In total disbelief, Silvia could only nod mutely. She could not trust herself to speak.

'That's where he fell. He couldn't remember exactly what happened but an old man and his dog heard him groaning and calling for help. He had fallen off the cliff and hit his head badly and must have been unconscious for a while. He survived, as he said, by the luck of the Irish. Apparently, no one should survive a fall like that, but he fell into some bushes on the side of the cliff and became tangled up in an old fishing net. I've kept the card ever since he told me that story. When he left Ireland, his aunt had given him a few of these cards for good luck. He gave some out and kept some. He's here tonight with my brother; I'll introduce you to him.'

Silvia broke into hysterical laughter and couldn't stop, she laughed so hard that she couldn't speak. A woman opened the door to go into the ladies but seeing Silvia's hysteria backed out again. Sally was confused and assumed Silvia was completely drunk. 'How can I help?' she asked, moving towards Silvia. Making a monumental effort to regain control, Silvia put out her arm to stop Sally getting any closer. She pointed to the door, gasping, 'It's …I'll be alright.'

Silvia was gasping for breath.

'Relax, Silvia, relax, breath it's OK.' Sally tried to calm her down.

'I'm, I'm, I'll be ….OK…. you go back to your party.'

'No Silvia, your not OK, come back to my suite. I wont take no for an answer.' Sally held Silvia by the arm and led her down the corridor through to the suite where she and Jim were staying. She could sense that something was definitely wrong.

'You rest here, while I go and find Nick.' Sally stroked Silvia's hair and reassured her that she wouldn't be long.

In that same moment Nick noticed someone who looked familiar to him. He couldn't place him at first, but knew he had met him somewhere before, the blue eyes and brown curly hair. Their eyes locked for a moment, the recognition was reflected in Pat's eyes as he nodded to Nick. Nick felt his chest tighten in disbelief, then someone tapped him on the shoulder.

'Hi Nick, I think you should know that Silvia is in my suite. She's not well and is very upset,' Sally said in a low voice, a look of deep concern on her face. She gave him directions and asked him to check on her.

Sean's memory was becoming clearer, he recognised Nick and the pieces of the puzzle were coming together. Nick had given him a lift and they had travelled to The Gap to see the scenery and stretch their legs. Sean liked Nick and tried to make a pass at him, only to feel an enormous thud on his chest. He slipped and was knocked unconscious. He awoke to a throbbing headache, moaning in pain, and no memory of how he ended up tangled in a fishing net on the side of a cliff.

He heard a dog barking and called for help. A man's voice called out to hold on, that he would be back with a rope. It was as if an eternity had passed until finally a rope came tumbling down towards him with a large leather strap. 'Put it under your arms and I'll pull you up.' He found out later his rescuer had mountain climbing gear and fastened the rope around a tree to winch Sean up to safety.

Sean stayed with the kind old man for a couple of weeks. His memories gradually started to come back. Not short term memories, not memories of Nick, but memories of his family back in Ireland and of backpacking around Australia. The old man was lonely as his wife had died four years prior. He enjoyed caring for Sean until eventually Sean was strong enough to continue his journey. He kept in contact with the old man and his family back in Ireland.

In another piece of good luck, he met John, Sally's brother, on Saint Patrick's Day in a bar in Melbourne. It wasn't long before they moved in together. When the laws changed so that gay men could marry, they did just that.

When Sean saw the car with the sign NicksCS at the clinic, memories of Nick came back to him. He wanted to know what happened, why did Nick leave him for dead, so he followed the car to the rural property. He assumed Rita was Nick's wife, all he wanted were answers but things got out of hand and now this poor woman was dead.

Silvia, now in Sally's luxurious suite locked the door as everything swirled through her mind. She had had a total panic attack.

She started laughing hysterically again. The thoughts of a wasted twenty something years, years of worrying and holding onto a secret that didn't even exist. All the fear locked in her body was flowing out like a champagne bottle exploding its cork and bubbling over. Her stomach muscles convulsed with emotion. All of the sadness, the secrets and the guilt were being released and she would be free.

In that instant, her whole life flashed before her eyes. She remembered as a child being taught to write, she couldn't understand why she was told to write her name from left to right, because she could see words from all angles, back to front, left to right, right to left, upside down and in mirror image. She was made to conform and forget all of her abilities, she could see other dimensions but through being forced to learn reading and writing, she lost all trust in herself. She no longer trusted her inner being and she began to look outward, listening to her parents and her teachers. She wanted to fit in, so she tried to be like everyone else.

She had below average grades and her parents were told that perhaps she was dyslexic and would benefit with extra help at school. She wanted desperately to be liked so she hid her own abilities and followed direction. All of her childhood abilities were now locked away somewhere deep inside of her.

Her dreams of being an artist were squashed. She didn't even remember loving art until she met Betty. She was told that artists don't make money and made up her mind to become a receptionist.

Her role would be set out for her: get married, have children and be content with that. But even those dreams weren't fulfilled because she was not able to have children. She had blamed Nick for the stupid accident that happened at the Gap. Sean wasn't even dead and they had wasted all those years feeling guilty and that they were being punished for not coming forward to tell the truth.

She knew it was her fault as much as Nick's. In a way she had used it to manipulate him; it was her way of keeping hold of Nick. They were bound together by a lie that had overshadowed their relationship.

She could see now how people played games with each other, one playing the villain and one the victim.

Her laughing eventually stopped and gave way to weeping, and when she was empty of all emotion she noticed she was timeless and weightless and everything was beautiful. In that instant she saw herself as everyone. Shocked and in awe, she realised it was all a play, a game in which she was all the actors. Everything merged into one, and there was no separateness, everything was melting around her and she could see waves like vibrations.

It was then she understood why she was working for Jim and Sally. The universe works in mysterious ways, she was meant to have closure, to know that Sean was alive, so that she and Nick could move on.

She knew what she was going to do: she would leave her job and pursue her art. She would also make sure that Sally knew about Jim's flirtations and what she saw Jim and Bob doing. She would no longer be a keeper of secrets.

In that timeless moment, she slowly looked up. Upon seeing her reflection in the mirror, her eyes with mascara running down her cheeks, she heard a knock on the door.

'Silvia, are you OK?' a familiar voice, Nick's voice.

Silvia exhaled and stared at her reflection, and there it was.

The perfect smile.

Silvia's smile.

Authors Note

If you enjoyed this book, please leave a review on my Amazon page or recommend it to a friend.

You can follow me on :-

Instagram
Facebook
TikTok

Diana_Nicolaci_Author

This book was inspired by *some* true events. I worked for various doctors and surgeons and also taught yoga for many years.

My husband kept a four leaf clover card in his wallet.

One of my students died in a terrible accident by falling into a ground level well. Was it an accident? We may never know.

the spirit of retribution is alive

Juliet

www.ingramcontent.com/pod-product-compliance
Lightning Source LLC
Chambersburg PA
CBHW032028240626
47154CB00003B/824